FIELD NOTES FOR
THE EARTHBOUND

FIELD NOTES FOR THE EARTHBOUND

A NOVEL IN STORIES

JOHN MAUK

Black
Lawrence
Press

Black
Lawrence
Press

www.blacklawrence.com

Executive Editor: Diane Goettel
Book and cover design: Amy Freels
Cover art: "Comfort Zone" by Bruce Holwerda

Published 2014 by Black Lawrence Press.
Printed in the United States.

ACKNOWLEDGMENTS

"The Earthbound," "The Blessed," and "The Insult Comic" originally appeared
as a chapbook, *The Rest of Us*, published by Michigan Writers Cooperative Press.
"The Moles" was originally published in *Third Wednesday*, "The Groundlings" in
Moonshot Magazine, and "The Tide" in *The Museum of Americana*. Thanks to these
fine organizations.

I am also grateful to some mighty mentors and comrades who influenced, nudged,
or shouldered this work in some fashion: Lee K. Abbott, Benjamin Busch, Bonnie
Jo Campbell, George Dila, Ferdi Hintze, Josie Kearns, Patricia McNair, Andy
Mozina, Holly Wren Spaulding, and Phillip Sterling.

For Karen

Contents

The Earthbound

Joel and Jeremy talked about Kathryn Mueller and the fact that she could fly. When the subject was anything else, anything but Kathryn, they worked like normal boys—ramming points at one another and huffing to conclusions. But Kathryn Mueller talks had gaps. And in the silence between words, each conjured a personal vision of flight. Joel's was purple. He'd see Kathryn up close, slicing through the air with cool gelatin darkness pressing into her face, the night curling out away from her shoeless feet. Jeremy's was faraway red. He saw Kathryn from a distance, like a dot arcing over the flatness of Northwestern Ohio and careening toward the Indiana horizon.

Kathryn was the orphaned niece of Bill and Sally Mueller. She had perfect hair for flying, no glasses, and the only green eyes in Blakeslee. She wasn't overly thick, but she didn't have the kind of body you'd associate with flying—plenty of bulk in the shoulders and plenty of circumference otherwise. Anyone familiar with Kathryn Mueller lore could dismiss it with a glance. And no one ever saw her fly—at least they didn't know it if they did. People didn't say, "Look! Up there! Isn't that the Mueller girl?"

Not seriously anyway. But Kathryn talked about flying the way others might describe a day at work—going up and surveying the fields, checking on people's affairs, detecting wind direction and telling anyone who might listen. Once, outside of Thiel's restaurant, after a quick dinner of meatloaf and sweet corn, she told two younger girls that clouds are like swimming pools, which made them laugh and walk away. And Kathryn gave reports: "Wilma Huddleston sits for hours beside her dog's grave." "Jackie Grundon fiddles himself behind his barn. He leans against the side and points it out toward the field." "Trent Leroy and Janet Brookins meet in the woods just after sunrise. They use a big tree stump." And so on like that. She didn't speak with an air of scandal. Her announcements were public notices—notes for the earthbound. But they had social impact. They put people into action. The Huddlestons got a puppy basset hound. Mothers grabbed their children's arms when Jackie Grundon came around. Bill Brookins divorced his wife and shot the windows out of Trent Leroy's house.

At the Nazarene Church, Kathryn made for hard work. Denying the claims of some secularist freak or godless Catholic would have been easy enough, but Kathryn was a member of the congregation. Every second or third Sunday, she'd enter the square brick building with her aunt and uncle. She'd parade down the aisle with an aloof sternness that adolescent girls were supposed to lack. Because her parents had died in a fire when she was only five, her abnormal confidence was attributed to shock or lack of guidance or both. After all, Bill and Sally Mueller were good Christians and decent farmers, but they were accidental parents, not the brisk certain types to guide a girl through the manifold opportunities of childhood. They lacked force. Also, Sally Mueller drove too fast. Her powder blue Chevy bulleted down back roads where only a few, but enough, farmers heard the RPMs howling over the delicate cornfield silence. It was no wonder Kathryn had loose ideas.

Joel and Jeremy were also Nazarenes so they got periodic eyefuls of Kathryn. They watched her stroll in, make her way to a pew, fidget with her unponytailed hair, and then casually head out the double doors to her aunt and uncle's car. She didn't tuck her chin into her neck like the other girls, nor did she acknowledge the tight-lipped whispers.

On a Sunday in April, when the adults were huddled in a prayer meeting and the kids were milling around in the post-church fresh air, Joel and Jeremy stoked up the courage to ask Kathryn point blank, "When do you normally fly?"

"I normally walk," she said.

"Do you fly at a regular time?" Jeremy asked.

"Do you walk at a regular time?" she asked back.

The boys didn't have the prowess to defend their questions—and neither had an affinity for talking to girls. They waited for Kathryn to walk away or call them something mean. She didn't. Instead, she settled into her spine, looked at one face and then the other with a warm smirk.

"So, what, you just fly whenever you want?" Joel asked.

"Whenever the feeling hits me."

"Do you feel like it now?"

"Nope."

"Why not?"

"It's only when I'm alone. Usually at night but sometimes in the morning."

They were just about to ask how—to get into the mechanics of it. Joel had the question ready. He was breathing in and forming the first letter when Bill and Sally Mueller emerged from the church. Kathryn said, "Gotta go," spun clockwise in the loose gravel, her dress swirling away from whatever legs were beneath it.

In June of 1953, word ran through Blakeslee and on up into Edon after Betty Morris found Kathryn in her hemlock bushes. Betty had gone out to hang laundry at first sunlight—because she believed it made clothes softer—when she saw Kathryn balled up with twigs and needles in her hair. "It was a crow." That's what Kathryn said to Betty from inside the bush and what Betty told everyone else. And most of all, the one detail repeated no matter who passed the story on, was the bloody clot above Kathryn's right eye where the crow's beak apparently pierced her forehead and sent her falling.

The pious wouldn't accept it. They reinforced their position, calling Kathryn truly sad. They reminded themselves about poor Betty Morris who'd lost her husband nearly five years prior to a sudden and massive stroke. "All that loneliness," they said. Others caressed the details of it all and wondered about sharing the sky with birds. As for Joel and Jeremy, they accepted Betty Morris's report like a news bulletin. They assumed Kathryn was on one of her nightly swoops and heading home at the first hint of pink when a surprised crow kissed her forehead. They imagined Kathryn and crow fluttering downward, each trying to regain composure while feathers twirled after their bodies.

"Crows're smart," Joel said. "You'd think he'd gotten outta the way."

"Yeah, if he'd known what to make of her."

"And if it was morning, he wasn't very awake probably."

"Can you imagine the look on his face just before they hit?"

On a muggy morning, after throwing rocks at a passing train, they decided to investigate—figuring that the crow, being smaller and more fragile than Kathryn, would have fallen to the ground after the mid-air crash. Out at Betty Morris's, they paced in rows like they were mowing the lawn. Joel took the front, Jeremy the side next to the field. Even a stray feather would have been enough. At one point, Joel thought he found something, a clot of bird parts under a lilac bush, and he called out. Jeremy came running and they stood ready for revelation, but the clot was the tail of a squirrel or some varmint—fur instead of feathers. They went back to pacing and scanning. By noon, they lost their gumption. If the crow had fallen, it wasn't there anymore. A cat or stray dog, they decided, could have come along. Or maybe the crow survived and managed to go about his business. Maybe he got the least of it. Maybe he and Kathryn hit at an angle. Or maybe a quick brush with a human skull wasn't enough, after all, to throw a full-sized and practiced crow into a tailspin.

Back home, a couple miles east of Blakeslee, Jeremy's mother refused to discuss it. She turned the conversation on Jeremy who was probably out gallivanting all day, dreaming up these sordid affairs instead of weeding around the barn. And his father didn't say much. Not that he was ever the conversant type, but he'd gone nearly mute two years back when his older brother put a shotgun to his mouth and pushed the trigger with a stick, apparently unable to overcome the grief of his oldest boy dying in Korea. "The Communists weren't worth it," he'd said before heading into the garage.

At Joel's house, Kathryn Mueller came up only once. A Saturday afternoon thunderstorm had caged them all in the livingroom. Joel was waiting for it to blow past so he could head out into the fields. His older brother, Tom, was watching horizontal rain out the north window. His mother sat crocheting in the rocker, and his father, Dale Krug—famous for drinking, wrecking, punching, and ruining things—stood in front of the screen door with his hands spread above the threshold daring the rain to come in. Tom said something about the Mueller girl getting blown all over the place. Joel explained that she wasn't stupid enough to be out in a storm.

"You think that girl can fly?" Dale asked.

Joel looked down at the carpet.

"Maybe. Ya never know," Tom said.

When their mother joined in, it was a family talk. "That girl has her own problems," she said.

"That doesn't mean she can't fly," Tom said.

"People don't fly, Thomas. You know better."

"Well, ya never know," Dale said out the screen door. "Ya never really know."

Later that summer, Joel and Jeremy got their second interview with Kathryn. After the last amen, they'd catapulted out of the muggy sanctuary. In the shade beneath the oak tree, they rolled up their church pants and splayed their legs across the grass. They watched Kathryn come down the front steps. She pulled the top of her dress a couple times to move air across her skin, scanned the churchyard, and walked straight toward them. When she got to the shade, Jeremy pushed his pant legs back down.

"Your dad drives the green pickup, right?" she said to Joel.

"Yep."

"Why was he sleeping out on County Road E the other night?"

"I didn't know he was."

"He was sleeping in the back, right there on the side of the road."

"You saw him?" Jeremy asked.

"With my own two eyes," Kathryn said.

"Were you out there or something"?

"That's how I saw him with my own two eyes." She kept looking down at Joel—waiting for him to comment.

He said nothing.

"Well, okay," she said. "I was thinking the mosquitoes probably did a number on him."

"Yeah, I don't know," Joel said.

Bill and Sally Mueller were headed their way, so Kathryn walked off. Joel and Jeremy sat in the fumes of it. They could both imagine a story that would put Dale Krug in the bed of his pickup out on County Road E. Since he'd thrown a pickled egg jar at the muttering owner of Ned's Bar, Dale had become a migrant drinker. He'd been showing up in different places, in different people's stories.

~

In September, the town's welcome sign was hit and knocked off kilter. People woke up on Sunday morning to the big blue greeting "Blakeslee: A Half Mile of Smiles" drooping toward the ground. At the Nazarene church, most assumed it was an outsider, a kid from Indiana or Michigan passing through on a Saturday night with his windows down and his head full of rock-n-roll music. Pastor Booth suggested it before service and that settled it.

Like usual, Sunday dinner at Joel's grandparents' started at 2:00. It was Joel, his mother, and sometimes Tom. Dale never came. He'd made it clear that formal worship and any church related dinners were his wife's, not his, form of salvation. And so Joel and Tom sat in the livingroom alone breathing the gravy aroma and waiting for their grandmother's cue to gather in prayer. Their grandfather had gone to pull the pan from the oven and move the big potato dish onto the table. All the comfort of his grandparents' house, or maybe the intimate scent of baked chicken, nudged Joel to speak up—to say what he'd been holding in for over an hour. "Kathryn Mueller said Dad was the one who hit the sign."

"When'd she say that?" Tom asked.

"Just today, standing out by the church. But don't tell."

"Why not?"

"I just don't think anyone should know."

"Why you talking to her anyways?"

"Jeremy and me, we sometimes talk to her."

Tom kept the secret for about eight minutes. At the table, after prayer and just before putting a fork of potatoes in his mouth, he let it fly. "So I heard who plowed into the sign." He didn't wait for a response and he didn't look over at Joel. "The old man did it."

"How would you know such a thing?" his mother asked.

"The flying girl told Joel."

"And how would she know?"

"Probably just looked down," Tom said.

Joel concentrated on the chicken. Other than compliments on the gravy, dinner stayed quiet. A month later, Dale moved out of the house for the second time. "And this time," he said, "I won't be back."

~

In late fall, public discussion about Kathryn Mueller climaxed when she was found face down in a field, her body pressed a good four inches into the mud. Some said she'd climbed the silo and jumped. It was a good theory, given her public musings, but her body was a full fifty yards from the silo and facing toward it, not away. Even if she could jump like a frightened white tail, it didn't add up. Others suggested earthly foul play—all kinds of fiendish corporeal stories that zipped past Joel and Jeremy's ears. But any rendering that got Kathryn planted into the hardening mud, with no footprints around, didn't make much sense. To Joel and Jeremy, it was clear to anyone who'd admit it: Kathryn Mueller could fly. It was only a matter of why anyone who could lift off the flatland and go shooting through the darkness on her own power would stop over the middle of a field. They wondered what bird, bat, or miscalculation would halt forward movement and let gravity do its terrible work.

"Maybe a sneeze," Joel said.

"Maybe," Jeremy decided.

Dale came back, staggered around for a year, disappeared again for a few months, and returned a final time to drag his family to a listing shack on the outskirts of Edon. While Joel tried to get traction in a new town, Jeremy orbited Blakeslee alone. He started smoking and stopped attending church. Both boys went sailing into the craven world, and they both remembered, in their own quiet, nights of squinting up, almost seeing something bigger than a crow or a goose, but neither ever conjured up the real rush of flying: the flavor of all that air. They didn't imagine Kathryn Mueller keeping her mouth slightly open so the wind could slip in around her teeth and dry out the inside of her cheeks. They didn't imagine how the business of everyday life churns out a lush perfume, how the breath of every person, plant, and animal marries together, works its way upward. They didn't imagine how the sweeter tones cluster just above the trees, how everything goes tart and brittle higher up, or how the best possible mouthful comes from swooping quickly downward from sour into sweetness. They didn't imagine any of that. But they were just kids.

The Blessed

My mom was a witch. I don't mean a New Age earth goddess or Wiccan. She wasn't a peacenik or spiritualist. And she wasn't retaliating against other religions. Back then, on the open flatlands of Ohio before the turnpike brought the rest of the world zooming through, being a witch was private business. It wasn't something to talk about or parade around. And it wasn't a choice any more than your last name. My mom was a real witch. She did things to people. She made things happen. And I can be honest now that she's gone. She's the reason David Manville looks like he'll eat your head if you give him half the chance, and probably the reason he molested that Jonas kid years ago, and why he went off to prison and did unspeakable things behind bars.

Yesterday, I saw David Manville in the grocery store. He's out of prison and back here buying bread and canned green beans like any normal person. But he's not normal. He'll never be normal. If destiny stumbles and he has children, they'll never be normal. I tried not to stare but couldn't help it. There he was—thirty-some years older, no longer the wiry eighteen year-old with stringbean arms. He'd become a thick-shouldered hunk of scowling meat—an animal caged in its own skin. It's odd enough seeing a guy like David Manville walking around in the world. It's odder yet to see him standing in a checkout lane holding groceries. It's like seeing a tiger with a birthday cake.

I was in Natalie Tolaski's lane, which meant I'd be standing there a while because she picks up every item, looks at it, comments, and then pushes it toward the bagger. I'd taken a step—hoping to jump over a lane—and that's when I saw David. When our eyes met, he didn't blink, turn away, nod his head, or anything. I pivoted back and looked straight at the person in front of me. I tried to shut off my peripheral vision and protect the side of my eyeball, but I could feel his stare. He was in Dana Trumbull's lane, so he moved ahead and I felt the air around me relax. I looked over and saw apelike bulges beneath a thin green t-shirt. Whatever had happened to him over the decades made his shoulders balloon up and cancel out his neck.

He must have just gotten back because I would have heard. The whole town would have heard. Even though it's been years, plenty of people from those days are still around. Plenty know the story—how he invited Billy Jonas into his house, took him upstairs, cornered him, pulled out his member and rubbed it on Billy's face. When the police came, David wouldn't go down to the station, not willingly anyway. It took four officers to carry him out—screeching and flailing like a stray cat. He was sentenced to three years, which didn't seem like much. But he did things and kept doing them. He was violent. Mrs. Jonas kept up on his campaign of prison assaults. She wanted to know when he'd get out. But years went by. Eventually, we all figured he was gone for good.

And it wasn't just David Manville. He wasn't the only target. My mom's curse washed over that whole family. His younger brother, Randolph, developed a condition in his teens or twenties that made him loafy and empty-headed. And the youngest, Melissa, threw fits. She'd go berserk right on the street, in the store, wherever. I remember seeing her drop to the pavement once. The family was crossing the street and down she went, gyrating against her mother's attempts to stand her up. When she got old enough, she married little Sammie Johnson and they beat each other senseless. You could go by their place any time of day and hear it. Somehow, in between punches and takedowns, they managed to have three kids—all of them, as far as I could tell, untamable. Nathaniel, the oldest boy, killed a woman on a bike. He wasn't much beyond sixteen and fresh behind the wheel. The police said he drove right over her, circled around in the field, left her body in the ditch, and drove back home. He's still away at some detention center.

And then there were the Polks. They got the curse as well. Marianne Polk died slowly. Back in the old days, she was a shrewd woman—the kind who had something to say about everything. But eventually, all her clarity evaporated and she turned into a crazy-haired open-mouth zombie. The family didn't have the money to take care of her in the right way and didn't have the sense to put her someplace safe, so they locked her up in her own bedroom. And like my mom used to say, if you're hoping to lock something up, you're better off killing it. Well, Marianne Polk managed to escape on a regular basis. She'd show up all over town—most often in her nightgown, but once, she walked stark naked down Main Street. It was August so there was plenty of flesh around—a few shirtless men, people in shorts—but no one expected to see Marianne Polk's whole body in all of its eighty year-old translucence. Lester Pollick, the gentle guy that he was, hobbled into the street, grabbed her hand and pulled her to the sidewalk. Gerald Polk's brain must have done somersaults when he found his wife on a casual bare-butt stroll with Lester. That winter, Marianne wandered into the fields. She fell down, snapped her leg in two, got pneumonia, and that was that.

The Polk kids—Lily, Leonard, and Ellie—were roughly my age. All within a few years anyway. Lily got around to marrying some guy from Hillsdale, Michigan. They had two children. One died from crib death and the other got some mental sickness that made her eat everything in sight. She swelled up to 400 pounds before a state agency came in and took her away. I don't know where she is now—if she's in a hospital or if she ate herself to death. Leonard moved down to Bryan, bought the local racetrack, and got himself tangled in underhanded business. He's long gone, but Ellie's still in a duplex over in Edon. She got married to a man named Nelvin or Nevin Shirky, had a baby, and left him to raise the girl on his own. I've seen Ellie around, and I can say without a doubt that she's as unhinged as any creature walking. She wears so much makeup that it's hard to tell where things begin and end.

The Housmans didn't fare any better. Maybe they were collateral damage. It's hard to say, but I know that Paula Housman lost her husband right after Mom delivered the curse. His name was Robert but everyone called him Red. He had a sharp jaw that made him seem important. He was the only Nazarene that accepted everyone—even the Catholics and even my mom. I remember hearing the story a few different ways, but the gist of it was a car killed him. He was under there working—because that's what people did in those days—and the jack gave way. Paula walked out the back door and saw his legs sticking out. It took a while before a neighbor made sense of her screaming, came around, and jacked the car back up. Of course, it didn't matter how long it took. The initial collapse pressed the top half of Red Housman into the ground. I heard the details about extracting him—or most of him. Out of respect, I'll keep those to myself.

So the Manvilles, the Polks, and the Housmans got the brunt of the curse. There may have been more. The Krugs, Smiths, Laneys—all those people and all their children may have caught some flecks of it. I'll never know. But what I do know is that Barbara Manville and Marianne Polk brought out the worst in my mom. They let loose something they couldn't imagine.

It all started with my sister. But it wasn't her fault. Martha couldn't help that she drove boys crazy. I suspect it was that cornsilk hair and how it trailed behind her when she'd walk through town. She streamed along like a fallen leaf on a quick current. You look away for a second and can hardly believe the distance. At fifteen, she was plenty fidgety. When the weather was good, she orbited town several times a day. She moved and kept moving. And no matter how you look at it or who you are, that's bound to attract attention.

So it was late May—a morning thick with honeysuckle and lilac. Martha was at the churchyard talking with the Nazarene boys while their parents finished up churchy business. According to the story, she got to kissing with Leonard Polk behind the big lilac bush. The minister looked out the window and saw things happening—Martha and Leonard going at it while a few other boys watched. When Barbara Manville and Marianne Polk came to our house, they were still in full church garb. I looked out the front door and saw them whispering. I let them finish, straighten their dresses, and knock. I answered and called for Mom.

"Lorna, we have to talk," one of them said.

They went into the livingroom. Mom was a good host. She always said that if someone comes to your home, no matter what, you bring them all the way in. You let them into the center of your life. That way, you get past all the doorway niceties. Mom hated niceties.

I stood in the kitchen just past the threshold. I knew something was going on because nobody from the Nazarene church had ever been to our house. The women sat on the edge of their chairs and neither wanted anything to drink, not even a glass of water. They kept sighing. They said Martha waltzed into the churchyard and riled up their boys.

"So your son was kissing Martha?" Mom said.

"It wasn't just kissing, Lorna."

They were insinuating things. They explained that it was some kind of show. One of them said something about perversion, which was the first time I'd heard that word. The conversation went on and on. They talked about their beliefs, their families, and the clear difference between right and wrong. For them, it was more than teenagers exploring romance. It was about sin and Jesus and the proper way to wear one's hair. Somewhere in the middle of it, Martha came in the front door and glided past them. That's when Barbara Manville made a point of telling Mom to keep her hussy daughter away from the church and God's children. It was deliberate. She wanted Martha to be ashamed. And that's what changed everything.

I remember watching the dust—how it writhed in the big sunbeam—and how Mom looked at me when I shifted my weight and made the wood creak. She turned back toward Barbara Manville and started whispering—that choked kind of whisper that comes from clenched throat muscles. She told them to leave. The women got up in a hurry, and just as they reached the front door, Mom said it clearly, like she was telling them the time. "You will always regret this."

Until then, I hadn't witnessed anything dramatic at our house—nothing torrential or abrupt. I suppose Mom's power, which she once called her mother's "tradition," worked quietly in our lives. Her garden was always lush, no matter what the weather did. I remember a drought year. Everything went yellow and shriveled. The farmers lamented their corn and soybeans. I'd walk through town and see tangles of pale weeds where gardens should have been. Even Lester Pollick's garden, three houses down, looked like a thin blanket of straw. And then I'd get here to our place—to our double-size yard, the last one before the town spills into open fields. I'd come around the wall of hemlock and into the shade of our huge cottonwood. I'd smell the clay and minerals and see Mom's garden—a jungle of green sturdy herbs, vines, and stalks announcing themselves against a backdrop of thirst and privation.

And we had the dogs, Dilly and Tobias, our scouts and onlookers. Besides the local horses and cows, they were the biggest four-legged creatures around. They were Irish wolfhounds or something like it. When I was young, they were walls of moppy hair—panting over the top of me, shouldering me toward the back yard. They lived until I was twenty-five. Once I asked Mom how old they were. She said, "They're very old but very healthy, Jacob." Those dogs did everything Mom said, as if they had some direct connection to her thoughts. And they didn't do any of that dumb dog stuff—barking their heads off or writhing against a chain whenever someone walked by. They were dignified. If they needed to bark, they did so, but only once or twice until they were convinced Mom had heard. She'd acknowledge them and that was that. And when we came home from school, they'd each come up, lick us once in the hand, then go back to their business. The few times I got huffy as a kid—anywhere close to a tantrum—they were right there looking down, almost shaking their heads, tssking.

And we ate well. While most other kids choked down brown and white glop saddled up next to a hunk of bologna, we ate a spectrum of roots, greens, and spiced breads. Mom knew how to pull flavor from the ground. My mouth got accustomed to richness and contradiction—all kinds of fluffy egg concoctions, creamy potatoes, heavy stews that were sweet enough to be dessert. If we ate something from a restaurant, which was rare, it tasted flat, and the candy sold at Kaiser's grocery tasted like detergent. And I can still barely stomach any of that prepared food that goes into your freezer. It's like licking tar off the road.

I never got sick as a kid. Neither did Martha. We didn't get the standard shots. I didn't even know about inoculations until my thirties—when my girlfriend at the time looked at my arm and noticed the missing dimple. There we were in bed. She started pulling at my skin and inspecting. She asked where the scar was. I told her I didn't really know, which was true, and we got back to business. This year I had the flu for the first time, which made me feel sorry for people who've had it more than once.

But even so, our house wasn't all that strange. That's my point. Sure, there was the garden, the dogs, the food, the good health. Sometimes, I wonder how much she fended off—how many whispers or bad dreams or fevers. I wonder if she stopped bullies before they saw me, if she firmed up the ice before we ventured onto the pond, if she stopped the lightening or sent it off elsewhere. But even if she did, I don't think those Nazarene women knew anything. We dressed like everyone else. Martha and I went to school and did our work like the other kids. Mom didn't wear weird dresses or act odd in public. She was quiet, but not anymore so than a regular quiet person. She'd walk down by the river in the evenings, but that wasn't exotic. To anyone looking in from the outside, Mom was a non-religious widow with two children. That's it. And I suspect those women never figured it out. Given their notions about the world, they probably didn't imagine that Lorna Ferrick meant what she said on that Sunday. If they could have climbed out of their lives, if they could have elevated themselves enough to look down and see all the tragedy concentrated on their families, if they could have charted out the gnarled details, they might have concluded something about that day. They might have regretted coming to our house, demonizing Martha, or even listening when the minister told them what he saw. They might have remembered way back to their teen years when life forces tickled their own ribs and made them yearn in every direction beyond the church pew.

After they left, Mom came into the kitchen. She cupped Martha's shoulders and told her, "You're not anything those women will ever say."

"I know," Martha said.

Then we had canned cherries in syrup.

All that week, Mom murmured to herself. She spent nights by the river. Down in the basement, I saw a bucket filled with sludge. It sat on a stool for days. I could smell the dankness wafting up the steps. I looked in it once and saw nothing but frothy mud. I knew it was for something important. After a few days, every room in the house smelled like the river—like wet roots and decay. We didn't talk about it though. We went about our business and lived in the murky scent of the St. Joe.

A week after the Nazarene women had come and gone, Mom brought the bucket upstairs. I saw her standing by the back door. She looked down into it, whispered, and then walked out. Part of me knew that I should stay home, but most of me wanted to

watch, so I followed. She traced the back lawns around town—
the bucket cutting through the long grass. When she cut in and
crossed over to the church, I stayed behind a tree. I saw her
walk up to the front entrance like she might go in and have
a seat. But she stopped, stood straight for a few seconds, concentrating or whispering or just staring. Then she brought the
bucket back and slung its contents at the door. The muddy foam
sprayed out against the siding. From across the street, it looked
like a wound—a brown gash. I don't know if it made a sound,
if anyone heard or saw it. If they did, they stayed in the pews
and kept worshipping. Mom walked back home, right down the
street, with the empty bucket dangling. Later that day, I heard
her sobbing in her room.

After that, Mom stayed in the house. She set up a garden in
the diningroom and kept the windows open to let the herbs feel
the wind. When we'd get home from school, she'd make us read
aloud from old storybooks, textbooks, even mathematics, which
I detested. She'd make me recite equations while she tapped a
rhythm on the chair. And once I read a whole chapter from my
history textbook, which made her double over in laughter. She
covered her face and howled into her palms. She kept saying,
"Don't stop. Keep going!" Every other paragraph or so, she'd start
up again. Dilly and Tobias stood beside her wagging—maybe
enjoying the sound of it all, maybe sharing a joke that I didn't get.
She showed us how to read upside down, how to use rainwater to
make tea, how to rub herbs in our hands and bring them to life.
She talked about that smell—when a leaf releases its scent into
the air. The whole world, she said, changes when that happens.

As soon as she was able, Martha left. She couldn't take the
hounding from the farm boys and their mothers. "Cows!" she
said. "I'd rather talk with cows."

She meandered around out West for a few years. Then, at nineteen, she fell in love with Canada and settled in the Alberta wilderness. She wrote letters and sent stacks of photos. Mom and I would sit in the livingroom—Dilly and Tobias at our side— waving to the mini Marthas standing in front of mountains and spiky northern trees. With each envelope, Martha's hair grew longer—and then way longer.

I went to school for a while, had a few jobs, a pretty good one in Toledo. Then I came back here to help Mom. The house seemed too big. Toward the end, she had me bring plants into her room. They were lined up on the floor and squeezed onto the shelves and dresser. They thrived in there and created a canopy above her bed. The bending stalks and arching branches eclipsed the ceiling. The air was thick with soil and plant breath. It was like that for a few years, and then this past spring, surrounded by vines and protruding leaves, Mom died. I went to her room in the morning and brushed the leaves from her face. She'd had a full life. Even though Dad died many years ago, right after I was born, Mom still had Martha, me, Dilly and Tobias. I once conjured up the notion that Dad and Uncle Ralph were inside those dogs—watching and panting and making sure.

Toward the end, I asked questions. I wanted to know about everything from the curse to the plants, where it all came from, who we were, why we lived on the edge of everything and every- one else. She'd tell me not wonder backwards. But I came to some conclusions of my own. I scraped back into history and found that our father was Irish—born of Ferricks and Tallys—that Mom came from Holloways and Muellers. She was double Dutch. There were some Muellers around, out toward Montpelier, but they're gone now. So it's just me—me and what I've kept around, what I've pieced together from memory and reflex. I don't have

Mom's force—her clarity and understanding. But I know some things. For instance, I know that all your senses can fool you—all except your nose, which sits there in the center and never lies. I know that plants are always reaching for us, that if we'd stay in one place long enough, they'd finally wrap their arms around us and welcome us home. And I know that plenty of people have been cursed. I can see how they lumber along, fighting against their own muscles and bones. I can tell just like a dog knows when you're sick and a horse knows about the winter ahead. I can see a curse from a hundred yards away—the greasy shimmer around all the effort. I also know that a curse drains something away from the person who delivers it. It's not quite like a bee giving up its stinger, but it's close. And once a curse goes out, it's gone. You can't take it back any more than you can stop a rock in mid air.

Two weeks from now, I'm going up to see Martha, her husband, and their two children, Dane and Veronica. It'll take days of quiet driving. I'll leave here, shoot up through Michigan, cross the big bridge and turn left. I'll go west and then slip north into Canada. I've done it every year for years. Each visit, Martha seems more like Mom, calm and balanced. And her home, a tiny cabin surrounded by dinosaur-sized pine trees, feels crowded with contentment and wonder. Her husband is a lofty Norwegian who talks to Martha and the children as though they're all pieces of sacred glass. They have three dogs that watch over the family like fussy mothers.

I won't tell her about David Manville. I doubt that it would translate. It'd almost take another language—as though these words, the ones we are using now, wouldn't work up there, as though the tragedy that haunts the Polks and Housmans and Manvilles would peel off and fall away. Sorrow belongs only in some places, only on the shoulders of some children.

The Repo Run

Warren Harlow didn't want the job at Grundon Furniture. He didn't want any job. But his mother insisted. She slid a sausage omelet in front of him, started buttering her own toast, and told him that he'd have to get work, real work, if he wasn't going to finish up at the high school. Warren sliced the omelet into chunks and watched the steam worm up and into the sun. He'd been expecting something from somewhere—a hand or hook to yank him back into public life. It had been a solid month since his father had died from a massive stroke in the back yard and going on three weeks since his principal explained the bereavement policy, which Warren saw as an exit sign—a polite but clean way to end the droning anxiety of high school.

"You can't hide out here forever," his mother said.

"I'm not hiding," Warren said.

"Call it what you like," she said back. Then she got up, went to the basement, and started a war on the past. For a string of days, she stayed up late, shuffled through crates, and threw out old clothes. Each morning, she lit the burnbarrel and filled the air with the stench of charred fabric. She made trip after trip to the end of the yard, committing armloads of clothes and hatboxes to the flames. From his window, Warren saw the heatwaves during the day and the finger of smoke in the morning. And he tried to ignore the fact that she'd been putting *The Bryan Times*, opened to the classifieds, on the kitchen table. Still, he had no choice but to look, and that's how he saw the Grundon Furniture ad. They wanted a warehouse assistant—someone to stock, move, and deliver. *No experience necessary. Strong back a must.*

On a clean morning in April, Warren stood in Mr. Grundon's office. He looked at the chocolate-colored desk that stretched from wall to wall, and he knew, like he knew the sound of his own name, that change was coming. No more high school—and good riddance to it anyway. No more bereavement. No more crisp mornings watching a bobber on Lake La Su An, and no more afternoons wandering the fields with Duchess, his meditative husky mix.

Mr. Grundon asked Warren's age and lineage, if he was, by any chance, related to Townsend Harlow.

"Townsend was my uncle," he said.

"Townsend was your uncle?"

"My father's brother."

"Well, Townsend was a good one."

"Thank you for saying so."

"And your father?"

"Passed away. Just recently."

"Sorry to hear it. Naturally?"

"Yes. Well, a stroke."

"Why don't you have a seat there?"

Mr. Grundon closed a drawer on his desk, got up, and walked to the middle of the room. He put long pauses between sentences, looked out one window and then another. He talked about the

Grundon family—commitment, mutual reward, building and supporting a community, farmers and city people alike. Sometimes, he'd look down and ask Warren if it all made sense. Warren said that it did.

"So, young man, you want a job?"

"Yes, sir," Warren said. "I believe so."

"Okay then."

Grundon Furniture had the biggest supply around. With a little collateral or none at all, people could rent full livingroom sets. Mechanics, waitresses, anyone who wanted could have upholstered chairs and matching end tables. *Everyone deserves the good life.* That was the motto. And Warren knew it plenty well. It was in the newspapers and on the radio between all the new rock-n-roll music. Furniture meant Grundon, and Grundon meant the good life.

Warren took to the job. In his first week, he loaded appliances, checked stock against charts, and wheeled merchandise to the front whenever sales people called back. He liked saying, "It's on the way." He liked the smell of the place—lacquer and varnish mixing with exhaust fumes. He also liked how Leo Warchol, the hairy-armed warehouse manager, drank coffee out of Styrofoam cups all morning and into the afternoon. By Thursday, Warren was doing it too—standing outside the back door just after lunch, holding the cup below his chin, and letting the steam moisten his upper lip. Warren also liked how Mrs. Grundon, who had the brightest lipstick he'd ever seen, would pull behind the shop, honk the horn of her giant '62 Plymouth, accept the hand of Leo or any of the warehouse men, and disappear into the polished showroom. And even though she was a little too polished for Warren's tastes, he appreciated her compliment: "Now there's a handsome young man with strong arms."

Warren read manuals and magazines. He marveled at the brands and wondered how fine European fabrics withstood the salt of the ocean. Even way down inside a ship's hull, there had to be some briny air seeping through. He wondered how much it cost to get a mirrored chest from Italy to America, how many ropes, hands, and foam cushions were needed, how many sofas and credenzas had been lost at sea, who would pay if a whole ship went down in a storm. And he thought that he might stay in the business for good. It was honest work. Everyone needed furniture.

At the start of the third week, he learned about the other part of the job. Leo told him to jump in the white truck—the one without the Grundon logo. "Let's you and me do the morning run," he said.

"What run?"

"The rescue run."

"Who needs rescued?"

"Furniture from nonpaying customers."

"Like repossessing?

"That's what some call it.

"Don't police do that?"

"Police?"

"Yeah, or someone like that."

"We're someone like that."

In the driver's seat, Leo studied the clipboard, turned a page and kept on reading. He laughed a little, started the truck, put his Styrofoam cup in the holder, and pulled out. He drove west to the outskirts and turned down a gravel road that followed the railroad tracks. Warren wondered if the furniture would be waiting, if people would invite them in, show them the right room, or point a weapon through a screen.

They went until the gravel turned to dirt and the fields turned back into trees. Leo slowed down as they came to a brown two-story in a half circle of poplars. He pulled past the driveway, yanked the wheel, hit the brakes, and backed up through the weedy yard. "There won't be anyone here," he said, "but if there is, let me do the talkin'. You just lift when I say, okay?"

"Okay."

"And stay out of any entanglements."

"Okay."

Behind the truck, Warren noticed the baseball bat in Leo's right hand, which made him want to walk up the dirt road and head for home. But he followed close as Leo crossed the porch, knocked on the metal slat door, waited, and then popped the wide end of the bat through the glass. The shards sprinkled onto the floor.

"Not the most polite method," Leo said, "but effective."

Inside, the walls were covered in photographs. They ran up to each corner, stopped for the grandfather clock, started up again, and lined the hall toward the bedrooms. Warren studied the rows of single bodies, each person standing on a porch or beside a giant tree. He wondered if they were cousins, ancestors, or children, if they were still alive or long since gone. He put his face to the wall, closed one eye, and saw the frames converge into a perfect line. Someone had used a string or made a line with a two-by-four.

"Hey," Leo said. "Grab an end."

"Sorry."

Warren kept looking over his shoulder and down the hall—expecting someone to charge out with a shotgun or hammer. They hauled out a sofa, a recliner, a coffee table, and two end tables.

"Done," Leo said.

"What about their door?"

"It'll be open when they get home."

"Is that it?"

"That's it."

The second stop was a ramshackle house out on County Road E. A feisty shepherd was tied to a tree and the front door was already ajar. The inside smelled like burnt grease. There were no photographs and the livingroom wall had two head-sized holes in it. They hauled out a floor lamp and a recliner with a puncture wound on the seat.

Heading back to the warehouse, with both windows down and the air whirling in a cyclone, Warren asked if they'd do the run every Monday.

"Most," Leo said. "And it seems like more all the time. People get caught up," he said over the wind. "They can't stop wanting. That's how people are."

~

By early summer, Warren was accustomed to pulling food out of refrigerators, yanking and heaving, clearing paths, leaving blank spots. He got used to curious and frightened dogs—tails wagging or stiff. And he even got used to people watching. Usually, they didn't protest. They knew the situation. They'd shrug, lean against a counter, jangle some silverware, or look for things that were long gone. Sometimes, they'd argue. They'd say they'd bought everything outright, that Leo's chart was wrong, that he was all full of shit, that he was a fucking burglar about to get shot. Some said they were gonna call the goddamn police. Sometimes, they'd get all the way to the phone and even pick it up.

Once Warren and Leo caught a man in Blakeslee, Marcus Johnson, standing naked in his kitchen—a mound of dough on the counter and flour everywhere. When Leo and Warren came to the door, he opened it, stood proudly, and showcased a fat old pecker in a brambly gray nest. Leo turned his head away and told Johnson to "clear out your fridge," which he did methodically—going back and forth with armloads of food against his pinkish stomach. Another time, Leo and Warren cleared a whole livingroom while the couple screamed at one another in a back hallway. The man said it was her fault for not keeping track of bills. The woman said it was his fault for having an affair with a huge-tittied waitress. Warren tried to ignore them and imagined the waitress was Rebecca Landers at the Uptown Café.

Sometimes Warren and Leo told repo stories at the warehouse but they mostly kept quiet. The shame, the heft—something about some lives—came back with the furniture and hovered around. It created a silence. Warren said nothing about the wide-eyed boy in pajamas who defended his home by throwing handfuls of plastic army men. He said nothing about a skinny woman in a bathrobe, Polk was her last name, crouching in a corner and hissing like a cat, and not a word about the young couple slumped in an unfinished kitchen, clammy looking and oblivious.

~

At home, Jake Leppelmeier had been coming around to help Warren's mother with financial matters. And Warren didn't mind. He felt okay about the somber old guy—the way he always stood up, shook Warren's hand, and asked how the new job was treating him. And on a Friday in late June, Warren felt okay when he came home to Leppelmeier's dandelion-colored Plymouth in the driveway. He pulled partway onto the grass and walked around to where Duchess waited. He nudged her aside and came in through the kitchen where he saw Leppelmeier's briefcase by a stack of bank statements and forms. On top was an insurance check for $34,287.98, more money than Warren had ever connected to anyone. He wondered if it was some kind of financial language that he didn't understand, a figure projected out over a hundred years. He looked at it hard. Then he heard his mother's voice. She was shouting. And it made Warren head through the livingroom toward the stairway. He heard it again, guttural and gritty like how she'd yell at Duchess to get off the carpet. He felt his brain groping. He went up one step, then a second. He imagined trouble but couldn't give it shape. He wondered if he should sneak up quietly or run full throttle. And then again, his mother's voice rang out. This time, he could decipher words. "Get in there!" He took another step and wished for the first time in months that his father were alive. Halfway up the stairs now, he could hear a collage of other sounds—friction and breath and then his mother's voice again. "Get it in there! Get way up in there!" Warren focused on the last few stairs, and then he heard a long throaty vowel—the deep sound of gratification or surprise.

Outside behind the shed, Warren sat with Duchess and stared out over shin-high corn. He watched the woodpatch beyond the field fizzle into darkness and he figured he might as well get a small room in Bryan—an upstairs in one of those duplexes, maybe the kind with an outside stairway, something close to the courthouse where he'd fall asleep every night to traffic spooling around the square. Another couple of paychecks and he'd start looking.

~

On a Monday in July, Warren found himself in charge. Leo had broken a foot over the weekend in a roofing accident. It meant

Warren would read the chart, drive the truck, knock on doors, and carry the bat. It had to be done. Warren was the man for the job. Mr. Grundon said it straight. "You're the man for the job." So Warren went out back and looked at the big white truck. He considered quitting. He almost turned around, walked into Mr. Grundon's office, and told him in plain words that he wouldn't be a repo man anymore. He'd gladly stay on as an assistant, the best warehouse assistant anywhere, but he wasn't cut out for the other part. He just wasn't. And he was ready to say all that. He felt it knotting up in his jaw. But the new kid, Danny Baughman—a fast-talking teenager from Pioneer—came around the corner and said he was ready to go. "Mr. Grundon says I'm going with you!"

"Well," Warren said, "don't get in a yank."

At the first stop, they got a sofa and two end tables from an apartment on the west side because the woman, Geraldine Clark, had died after the third payment. Warren told the landlord he was sorry to interrupt the morning. The landlord said it was no problem and wished him a good day. The second stop was a brick farmhouse on Route 34. The customer was supposed to be at work. That's what the chart said: *Laney, Burt. Works Days. Recliner, Sofa, Two End Tables.*

"Burt Laney?" Danny said. "Crazy Burt Laney?"

"I don't know. You know him?"

"Not on a personal basis. But Burt Laney's crazy. And he's big as a horse. I'm telling you, man. He's big as a horse."

"Okay. Well, let's hope he's not home."

Warren backed into the driveway. He tried the front door and decided not to venture around back where a big-sounding dog was raising a ruckus. He took the bat and tried to make a little hole—just big enough for his hand to pass through. The pane cracked up the center and half fell into the house.

"Crazy Burt Laney's gonna love that," Danny said.

"Let's hurry."

They were loading the sofa when Warren heard the gravel. He looked down to see Danny's face go flat, went to the edge of the truck bed, and saw a pork-faced man getting out of a green Buick—a cloud of dust still writhing around. An alarm panged in Warren's head. He yanked down the back door, crawled over the furniture, and shimmied into the cab. Danny was already in the passenger seat yelling to start it up, Jesus Christ, start it up. As Warren slammed down the clutch, he got a glimpse of Burt Laney's squinty eyes—pale blue buttons relegated to the margins of his face. He pressed the gas and heard the engine wind up, but his left leg went rogue. The clutch inched back and then popped all the way. The truck lunged and stalled. Warren started it again and let the clutch out in short jerks. In the side mirror, he watched Burt Laney's reflection tremble and shrink away.

Along the curves of 34, the furniture shifted in the back. Tables from Geraldine Clark's apartment were banging against the walls, the door bouncing up and down. Danny kept saying, "Wow, man. Wow." And Warren kept looking in the mirror, thinking about the way Burt Laney grinned—calm, entertained, his lips like big comfortable nightcrawlers, his neck swollen or missing altogether.

~

A week later, Warren got a cup of coffee after lunch. He poured in sugar and went out to get some sun. He took a seat on a cinder block, leaned against the warehouse wall, and looked out. A green Buick trolled along the far edge of the parking lot—inching along where the pavement crumbled away into open fields. And there was Burt Laney's left arm hanging out the window, a hunk of white meat glowing in the sun.

The next day, it happened again. Warren was drinking coffee and scanning the fields when the green car came seeping across the horizon. It angled toward the warehouse and stopped—blurring in and out like a mirage. Warren tried not to stand up and run inside. He kicked his right leg out, wiped his pants, and leaned back. The Buick didn't move. And Warren imagined himself in a gunsight, targeted, his head nicely motionless against the wood siding. He got up slowly, stretched a little, dumped his final swish into the gravel, and slipped in the door. He spent the afternoon tightening legs in the loft.

The next day, he told Leo, who'd come back in the mornings. "A guy's been coming around. Someone from the repo list."

"Been coming around?"

"Driving through the lot."

"Who?"

"Burt Laney. Lives out on 34. We got some livingroom basics from him last week."

"You know it's him?"

"It's him."

Leo shrugged. "This kind of thing happens."

"Should we do anything?"

Leo looked around the warehouse, rubbed his arm hair, and said he'd let Mr. Grundon know.

On Monday, there was one stop. Larry and Mary Sturla, both home during the day, were supposed to have the sofa on the porch. They'd called on their own volition, hoping that someone could take it off their hands, at least for the time being. That's how Leo explained it. When Warren and Danny pulled up to the house, two longhaired mutts ran in tight circles by the tires.

And when Danny opened his door, one slithered into the cab and started licking—excited as hell for visitors. It took a few minutes for Warren to get out, get past the frolicking dogs, and gain his composure. He remembered one of Leo's rules: don't smile or frown.

Like the chart said, the sofa was waiting on the porch, a white sheet draped over the top. A dusty-haired man, apparently Larry Sturla, stood in the threshold. "Thanks for coming," he said through the screen.

"No problem," Warren said. He pulled the sheet off and revealed pristine upholstery.

"So, you'll just load it up then?"

"Yeah. We'll get it."

"Thanks. We can't finish the payments, not right now anyway."

"It's okay."

"We'll come back this winter, get another one, maybe something with leather."

"Okay," Warren said.

Coming back on 34, Warren let the hum of the road fill the cab and imagined himself with the power to determine who could keep the furniture. "You decide," Mr. Grundon would say. "You pick the good eggs from the bad." The Sturla's were good eggs. They'd kept the sofa clean. They had good dogs. And maybe Mary Sturla was sick or pregnant or working nights at a diner. Maybe the sofa was the only place to sit, the only comfortable thing in the house. They deserved some extra time, maybe even a discount. So did the mother with the kid who threw army men.

"I heard about Crazy Burt Laney," Danny said. "Apparently, he's been prowling around?"

"Yeah, he's up to something."

"Up to getting himself bushwhacked."

"How's that?"

"You cross Grundon, you write your own ticket."

"Ticket to where?

"A quiet place in the woods."

"What's that mean?"

"What do you think?"

"I don't know."

"Really?"

Warren concentrated on the wind sucking through the little triangular window, the warm air like cream smearing over his hand. "So," he said, "Grundon goes after people? Is that what you're saying?"

"He's got guys on the payroll."

"Like who?"

"Like the Hostler boys. Those goddamn lunkheads, they'll do anything for a few bucks."

Warren thought of an afternoon early in the summer—right after he got the job—when he and Leo showed up to a place east of Blakeslee where all the family's stuff was scattered in the yard. Two pieces of furniture waited for them in the driveway and everything else, from coffee cups to slippers, was thrown around in heaps. Somebody was getting evicted, and at least two of the Hostler boys were there flinging hangers, wearing women's underwear on their head, making a real show of it. "You're saying," he said, "that Grundon has the Hostlers go around beating up customers."

"Not customers, deadbeats, people who don't pay and won't give up the furniture."

"I don't know," Warren said.

"Man, where you been?"

"Working. Longer than you, by the way."

"There's even a couple sheriff deputies who get involved."

"Pffff."

"It's what I've heard."

"It's news to me."

"Doesn't mean it's not true," Danny said.

"Doesn't mean it is," Warren said back.

~

Warren was invited to join his mother and Jake Leppelmeier for dinner each night. "We'll have a plate for you," she said. But he heard the opposite in between the words—a suggestion to be gone more than not. So he tried to burn up time after work. He blasted down the county roads squaring off the farms, sat on the spongy beach of Lake La Su An until the sun went down, and he even meandered in Bryan looking for a place to blend in— somewhere to get a sandwich without feeling like a stray dog. He spent one evening at a clangy diner on Main Street where the waitress stood in the kitchen threshold and glared at him while he ate. He figured that he'd hauled something from her bedroom earlier in the summer.

On a soupy Friday evening, Warren found himself a stool at Polk's Raceway—a place Leo recommended. It was a bar and regular sitdown restaurant tucked into the corner of a cavern-ous cement room beneath the racetrack grandstand. It stood a few miles west of Bryan and stayed open later than anyplace in town. Even though the waitresses weren't exactly a pack of honeys, as Leo promised, they were plenty nice. They took their time, leaned against stools, and laughed at the ceiling. Rollo, the crewcut bartender, told rambling jokes that trailed into his own laughter. Warren listened, settled in, and ordered a cheese sandwich with bacon. He wasn't old enough for anything but beer, but Rollo said he looked like a vodka man and insisted that he try his special hot weather tonic with lemon juice. Warren stayed through the sandwich, a full plate of waffle potatoes, and three tonics before aiming his car home. The following week, he packed a fresh shirt every morning, changed in the parking lot, and ended his nights on the same stool.

The next Friday, a little past midnight, Warren came home to Jake Leppelmeier sitting at the kitchen table, a cup of coffee and a half-eaten piece of cake in front of him. "You know a big guy in a green Buick?"

"Maybe," Warren said.

"Whoever it is drove by a number of times."

"When?"

"Earlier. 6:00, 6:30. Going real slow—one way and then the other."

"Did he stop?"

"Nope. Just inching back and forth."

In the morning, Warren went to see Mr. Grundon. He explained that Burt Laney was bound to cause trouble, that it was all but certain, and that he feared for his mother's safety.

Mr. Grundon closed the door, walked back to his desk, and sat looking out the north window. He crossed his arms and talked about family—the kind that builds up over a lifetime. He said that Warren was part of the family now, that he and his mother were under the Grundon roof. But he also explained a little hitch. "It seems," he said, "that Mr. Laney is the sheriff's wife's brother, and that limits our range of responses. Does that make sense?"

"I think so," Warren said.

"Mr. Laney and the sheriff are close is what's been told to me."

Warren waited for more, for something to add up.

"But that doesn't change the fact that he can't go ramrodding around. He can't lash out or flirt with people's fears. That's not how it works, that's not the kind of community we want. It's complicated. What I'm saying is, the law is the law, but sometimes it has in-laws. You understand?"

Warren nodded.

"So let's give Mr. Laney another chance. We'll send someone out there to have a talk. Does that sound okay?"

Warren said that it did.

~

Danny smacked the dashboard at the news. "Sheriff's wife's brother? See? I told you. Didn't I tell you?"

"I don't know what exactly, but you told me."

"Grundon takes care of business the old fashioned way. That's what I'm saying."

"How would you know any of that?"

"I'm saying, this'd already be done if there weren't a family issue."

"You're outta your gourd."

"Least I have a gourd."

Warren adjusted the side mirror and wondered if Danny knew what a gourd was.

"I'm telling you," Danny said. "This proves it. Why would Grundon bring up the sheriff?"

"I don't know. I suppose Laney might get away with more than he might otherwise. Something like that."

"Even better is the sheriff knows the usual dealings. And he's not letting it happen this time."

"What usual dealings? I've been here all summer and haven't seen or heard anything. Nothing like what we you're saying."

"Maybe others have."

"The Hostler boys, right?"

"And sometimes a deputy or two."

"I'm still wondering how you'd know such a thing."

"Everyone does."

"If everyone means you," Warren said.

"Everyone but you," Danny said back.

At lunch, Warren stayed in the warehouse and drank coffee in the loft. He wanted nothing to do with Danny and his theories—about a showdown between Grundon and the sheriff, some longstanding feud coming to climax. It was all nonsense. He spent the afternoon polishing tables. After work, he walked to his car without looking at the horizon, then drove up to Lake La Su An where he sat on his hood, his feet on the chrome bumper, and counted the evening ripples—hundreds of bass sucking mosquitoes and flies down into the dark. And he decided, then and there, it was time to move on. He was untethered, not particularly needed. He imagined himself far away, Chicago maybe. If there was anywhere to go, it had always been Chicago. He remembered the time he and his parents drove through on their way to the Badlands—how he pressed his head against the side window and tried to see where the buildings stopped. He remembered his mother breathing out and his father's silence, all three of them humbled in their own way by the city's gargantuan legs. And he figured, sitting there on his hood, that his own memory was trying to make a point. You don't just remember things. You remember them for a reason. The Harlows had been dying in these fields for generations. His father, an uncle who shut himself in a garage with the car running, another uncle who drowned in the St. Joe, and his grandfather who died from some kind of tractor accident. And so, by god, Warren decided he'd catapult away—somewhere with big walls to break up the open space, a city with shaded streets, alleys, nooks, and long covered entrances. There had to be a thousand furniture stores, hundreds anyway, over in Chicago, and if he gave his credentials—head assistant to a manager back in Ohio—he'd have no problem. Soon enough, he'd be arranging stock in a warehouse five times the size of Grundon's. He imagined himself learning to drink wine or scotch, getting friendly with bar owners, shaking hands with people in suits, leaving generous tips. He imagined getting an apartment and a slim-waisted girlfriend. He saw the whole city wrapping its arms around him and pulling him in close.

On Monday, Crazy Burt Laney showed up at Polk's. And even though Warren stopped breathing for a stint when he saw the buttonhole eyes, he stayed put. His legs locked and his left hand went for the fork. Crazy Burt Laney drifted through the room, took a stool across the bar, and splayed out his hands like two raw chickens on a cutting board. Warren peeled through his options—hit the floor and shimmy into the kitchen, head for the men's room and lock the door, lunge over the table to his left, run out, and disappear into the fields. He considered whispering something to Cora—something about keeping an eye on the big guy across the bar. But that didn't make much sense. So he sat still and watched Crazy Burt Laney recline against the stool, as if this were all normal, as if he were just passing by. And Warren entertained the possibility. There were only so many places to be, only so many roads and so many nights until people circled into one another. But that idea fizzled when Warren got a straight shot of Crazy Burt Laney's face. It was a showdown. Sure as heavy August heat, as sure as anything anywhere.

Warren looked down at his sandwich, all that cheese bloating out on the sides, and decided that he'd look vulnerable chewing and wiping his mouth. He let it alone and took a long drink. Cora came around and asked if his stomach was knotted. He said he was fine, just cooling off.

"Want me to wrap up that sandwich? Save it for later?"

"Yeah, okay."

"I'll leave those potatoes for you to work on."

Warren figured he'd hunker down, wait out the whole situation—the whole night, another night after that, however long it'd take. Even if he lunged over the table and out the door, the parking lot was big and his car was a good fifty yards off.

"I'll do another," he told Rollo.

"Another hot weather tonic," Rollo said.

Across the bar, Crazy Burt Laney clunked his bottle on the wood.

"Another for you then?" Rollo said.

Crazy Burt Laney nodded and Warren remembered the face of Scott Nicholson—a neckless deadeyed kid who once beat Warren's friend, Mark Dunham, into the ground and then made him lick a tree for half an hour after school. Warren remembered how Nicholson stared at him for days after that, how he leered across the classroom, aimed all his deadeyed energy so Warren would know he was next. It never happened. Nicholson never launched his attack, but he made Warren bite down on worry for a whole school year.

Crazy Burt Laney guzzled the second beer, grinned after a hard swallow, and nodded at Warren—in agreement or confirmation or something else. He pushed some cash forward, slid his stool back, and left.

"I'll take another," Warren said.

"Gonna stick around for a bit?"

"Sure," he said. "Sure will."

When the drink came, Warren held it up, nodded at Rollo, and took a long sip over the ice. "What do you know about Grundon Furniture?" he said.

"Everyone deserves the good life."

"That's right. What else?"

"Well," Rollo said, "Never went there myself. Have some family who got a livingroom set. They like it. So no complaints, I guess."

"Everyone deserves the good life," Warren said.

"That's right," Rollo said back.

Another hour went by. Others at the bar trickled out. Cora took off her apron, got a whiskey sour, and started stacking glasses.

Rollo called it a night. "Gotta shut'er down," he told Warren.

"Take that sandwich," Cora said. "And best stay off the main roads."

"Yeah," Rollo said, "go easy."

There were two paths north from Polk's—up 576 or the back way along County Road 10. He chose the back. Maybe he'd park at the Johnsons'—in the tall weeds behind their barn—and then walk home across the field. Maybe he'd eat the cheese sandwich while wading through their soybeans. And moving along through the dark, his headlights still off and wet honeysuckle air slithering around his arms, Warren decided he'd leave the first thing next week. He'd get a final paycheck, then shove off. It was time. His whole life was bucking and kicking. Everyone would wonder, but he'd write back soon enough. He'd explain the new job at a fine Chicago furniture store—a place that doesn't do repos because the customers can afford to pay up front. He'd tell about cruising around at the feet of skyscrapers and drinking with city people, about freighters bringing stock in from Italy and France, the mountains of credenzas stacked two stories up. He'd end by telling his mother to say hello to Jake Leppelmeier. He pictured them sitting in the kitchen, the letter between them, both nodding and awed at Warren's muster. And he imagined another letter to Grundon's—how Leo would smile over his coffee, that Danny would smack his own leg and figure, well, Warren was probably right about a few things. He let the possibilities jig in his head and light up the future. And in that last flash, just when he'd made out the edges of the big green Buick blocking most of the road, after his arms whipped the wheel hard to the right, Warren decided that he could clearly see Crazy Burt Laney standing on the berm, cattails stiff behind him. There was enough moonlight or starlight or ambient glow from all the light everywhere. It was him, those buttonhole eyes and hammy face directly ahead.

After impact, Warren studied the uneaten cheese sandwich smeared into his crotch. He figured it was a lost cause. There were other considerations. He pulled his head from the steering wheel and saw how the moon had slid into a clearing, how a chalk-colored film coated the trees along the riverbank. Other than the occasional tick from his cooling engine block, there was nothing, no breath, chirp, or night wind. And in that stillness, Warren felt forgotten, freed from memory—like some mammoth hand had opened, all the fingers curling back and away, the emptiness above him ready and waiting.

The Electric Nowhere

Nobody knows what happened at the racetrack—how the fire started, who started it, if Joel turned into smoke and blew away or if he got out. For weeks afterward, I hoped he'd show up smirking through the screen. I hoped myself sick. But the weeks turned into months and the hope turned into an ache that reeled out over decades. And the truth is, Joel wasn't the only one who disappeared. Back then we were all drifting away. That's how I think about it. One by one but almost all at once, people started leaving wherever they were. They walked, drove, hitchhiked, and married their way out. Sometimes, it was only a few miles, other times a state or two, and occasionally it was a complete mystery. It didn't matter where people stopped, had children, and grew old. Everyone was evaporating. Maybe that's my particular rumination, but I think I'm right about it.

For Joel, it must have started the day he came home to find his family's belongings smeared out over the yard. Like normal, I was with him. We never had a plan, just a shared notion that we'd boondoggle until dark. As we came out of the last woodpatch, we saw the row of cedars walling off the Krugs' dingy two-story. From a quarter mile away, the place looked normal, like an old tree stump, but when we got to the rim of the yard, we saw the contents of Joel's life spilled onto the grass, and I realized for the first time that the Krugs were everything I'd heard—wayward, twisted, stuck neck deep in every kind of hardship. Bland afternoon light brought out the shabbiness of their lives: pancaked couch cushions, scratches on the end tables, mismatched dishes, ratty blankets, several bruised coffeepots, chipped cups, toothbrushes with flattened bristles. Lamps had been dropped on the grass, the cords uncoiled and strung out. Piles of clothes were flopped on top of pots and pans. Dresses stretched across the livingroom table. Joel's boots, the soles caked with mud, sat on a small tower of sweaters, and linen-like shorts were piled on a stack of plates.

"Judas Priest!" That's what Joel said, which is a pretty funny thing to say when looking at your mother's bloomers in the sun. Of course, he wanted to scoop it all up and shove it inside. He wanted to but couldn't. The house was sealed tight and the locks had been changed.

I stuck around long enough for Joel's parents to show up and that was its own kind of trouble. Like every kid in the vicinity, I had orders to avoid Dale Krug—to stay outta arm's reach, to come straight home when he was around, and so on. But Dale Krug was everywhere, like wind, like a bad smell. He'd worked for the railroad, a body shop out on 34, at Hagger's meat store, in the Montpelier grocery. He'd also been a night watchman for the train yard and a driver for a machinery company over in Pioneer. His stink was on everything. And all along the back roads, he left a debris trail of Old Crown bottles—hard little reminders of his disdain for all creation.

Dale's green pickup came rocking into the driveway and stopped before hitting the kitchen table. Joel's mother got out first. She started grabbing and folding and re-stacking while Dale paced and yelled. He made promises to hunt down the landlord and strangle his pig fucker thugs. He sermonized and spit at pansied men who couldn't face him in direct fashion and who'd be feeling his foot on their throats before tomorrow. We watched and waited, and I swear I could see the words flying above him—wicked things with stingers designed for nothing but hurt. And then—as though everything rotten was ordered up from hell's latrine at that particular hour—the rain came. Any other time of year, weather on the flatland takes days to make up its mind. A storm will hem and haw and mope around in circles for days. But in the spring, it comes blasting in from Indiana like a big sneeze, and that's what happened. It turned Dale into a monster. He let out some dying animal sound, ran up the porch, threw his body at the door, and crashed it in. Then he barked something from inside, something quick and hoarse that sliced through the rain, and we jerked into action. We grabbed, scooted, and tucked what we could under our jackets, but it didn't matter. Within a few minutes, the stuff was drenched.

"Goddamn all the world," Dale kept saying. "Goddamn all of it."

We dumped everything in the livingroom, all but an orange recliner. Through the window, I saw Joel and Dale wrestling it up the steps, the reclining mechanism kicking and collapsing against their effort. Joel kept dropping his end and I felt that lull you feel when time hits the brakes—when everything and everyone plunges into syrup. Dale had had enough. He dropped his side, reached out, palmed Joel in the face and flung him

backwards off the porch. Joel's body launched, arced out, hit
the ground, and skidded to the center of the yard. There was no
cause, no effect, no father, no son. It was all one thing—a whoosh
of cruelty that had been waiting in the world for its moment.

Joel lay there letting splotches of rain smash him in the face.
When I ran out and bent over him, he looked through me at the
sky. I didn't ask if he was okay. I knew he wasn't. Dale went to
his pickup and blasted off.

I helped coax the chair into the house and then walked home
across the field—looking back through the rain, watching the
place shrink, wondering how Joel would get dinner, where he'd
sleep, how they'd manage the mess, how Joel and his mother
would fight off the thugs or Dale or both if any of them came
back. I wanted to get my father's shotgun out of the basement,
walk back across the field, and sit watch all night. I wanted to wait
on that porch cocked and loaded—one meanass kid with a gun
ready to make a messy hole in somebody. I wanted to but I didn't.

~

My mother had plenty to say about the twisted family across
the field. When I was younger, there were shrill whispers in the
kitchen. I got older and heard the nuances, which I already knew:
Dale was a menace who'd bury his family in hardship. Rebecca
was a quiet faithful woman who'd spend her life digging out.
Joel's brother, Tom, had already flown the coop—dropped out
of school, stole a few cars, got tangled in legal problems, and
then skipped on up to Michigan. The whole clan was biblically
bad-off, a verse out of Leviticus. But when it came to Joel, the
talk softened. One time, I heard my mother say that Joel had his
mother's reflexes. That wasn't true, not even close, but I appre-

ciated the effort. My parents knew that I needed Joel around. Because my sister died at two, I needed somebody. I would have been alone out there, surrounded by cornfields and grief and monsters of every sort. If it hadn't been for Joel, I would have been a maniac. That's the truth.

I never heard the financials of it, but Joel and his mother were allowed back into the house. Somebody made some concession or payment. No matter how it worked out, they cleaned the mud, washed the furniture, and the place felt healed up. Someone even repaired the splintered threshold. And for the rest of the school year, Joel and I spent afternoons hanging around with no fear of Dale who'd spiraled off on a long-term binge. We'd get root beers in town, carry them to Joel's porch, and savor the caramel froth in those golden hours before the sun fell into the fields. I remember how the wall of cedars would glow and how everything beyond it would turn purple and faraway. One time we sat there and watched my parents' goat go motoring along the horizon. We should've gotten up and chased it, but we didn't. We let that stupid goddamned goat head off to oblivion. After the umpteenth time of chasing it down and pulling it back to our barn, I decided that a cold root beer was more important. "Fuck you, James!" I said, which is what I called him, and Joel laughed himself onto the grass because that was the first time either of us had gone profane. It was also the first time we let something bad happen.

In the middle of summer, we came across the field and there sat Dale's pickup—backed in, its grill aimed out and menacing. It meant the end times—pestilence, locusts, gnashing of teeth. I invited Joel back to my place and he stayed through dinner. He sat where my sister would have, in that fourth chair against the window, and filled our diningroom with the exotic sound of dinner conversation. He popped the silence to ask how the potatoes got so creamy, and I could tell that my mother was flummoxed, not that anyone would like her potatoes but that someone would ruin the morbid quiet. Out of sheer politeness, she explained her recipe and pretty soon we were all discussing potatoes—where they come from, how they grow, even why they compliment a hunk of meat. My father, who was nearly mute, put entire sentences together between bites. Over dessert, there were more questions, theories, and a few points about butter and its many uses.

I told Joel to stay the night. I told him all kinds of things, but he figured a reckoning was inevitable, that his mother was over there alone with Dale and whatever business he'd brought with him. "I'm going back," he said. "Might as well get it over with."

"Might as well not," I told him.

"Easy for you to say," he said.

So he walked across the field, and I watched him dissolve into the dark. I don't know what happened, but I know it wasn't good.

The pickup started showing up every week and then all the time. On those days, Joel and I spun off. We explored the town, the fields, anyplace but home. That was a mantra—anyplace but home, anyplace but home. We'd convince ourselves that it wasn't dark, that it wasn't raining, that dinner was less important than seeing whatever needed seen. We talked little of our own lives because we lacked the words. We focused instead on the weather, the northern lights, the fox population that seemed on the rise, Indian ghosts that shimmered in the distance just after sunset, cows in the area that were always getting hit by lightning, and Kathryn Mueller, the Nazarene girl who could fly. That's the one that stayed with me. I used to lie awake at night imagining her liftoff. I wondered about the shift from one type of being to another—mammal to bird, human to angel. I'd think of her like a dot in the night sky, freed from her own weight. I imagined her swooping at trees and rocketing through the night air. And I always wondered what sent her crashing down into that field just north of her aunt and uncle's place. Once Joel said something that stuck with me—and maybe it was something from Dale's mouth. It had his tone. "Flying only counts if you can keep flying."

At the end of summer, I walked across the field and saw the pickup with its bed full of stuff. I stood in the corn—a row or two back—watching Dale shadow box a floor lamp. It was just him out there doing his thing, a lone animal with no pretense. I knew nothing about the formal study of lunatics, but I knew deep down that he was something with a label, something worthy of lab coats and microscopes.

Joel came out eventually and we met by the cedars. He said it straight. "We're leaving."

"Where to?" I asked.

"Edon," he said.

I could tell he'd been crying, and I could tell it was all sudden and foul. Dale had come along, charmed or bullied forgiveness from Joel's mother, and decided to move the family north and westward. "Goddamned new place has an outhouse," Joel said. "A goddamned outhouse."

~

So Joel went off to a falling down shack, a lean-to really, between Edon and Montpelier. He attended the Edon middle school, fought off Edon bullies, and slept among field mice. We were separated by twenty horizontal miles—planets for boys like us—but we still had Jesus. Once or twice each week, we met, as we had for years, at the mighty Church of the Nazarene. On Sundays and plenty of Wednesday nights, we'd sit in the pews,

fake sing, and wantonly deride the solemnity of prayer by opening our eyes and looking around the room. We'd shoot fake
boogers and wait for Pastor Booth to draw out the syllables of
some Old Testament condemnation—something about lechery
or lecherousness or thine iniquities. Like most boys our age, we
worked our way to the back pews, each week flirting with the
final lunge—some Sunday when we'd fling ourselves, forever and
ever—amen, out the double wooden doors and into the craven
world. And eventually it happened, but not the way we wanted.

For years, Myrna Underwood had attended every service with
her daughter, Tina, who was mentally retarded. Always in a flow-
ery dress, her thin hair striping her scalp, Tina would let out nasal
bawls in the middle of a sermon and send shock waves of loneliness through the sanctuary. She'd do it whenever Pastor Booth
raised his voice in drama—as though she were howling with him
in some primal language. Most of us pretended to ignore her.
We'd clench our bodies and let the reverberations dissipate. Even
Myrna Underwood maintained her posture, her shoulders tight
against the sadness. Of course, Tina was an easy target for asshole
boys like Eric Watson and Teddy Wingartner. Sometimes, they'd
leave her alone. Other times, they'd hassle and poke at her.

On this particular day, Joel and I were milling outside the
threshold. A few others gathered around—a gaggle of Nazarene
boys and a few restless girls shaking off the sermon. Myrna got
caught in a conversation inside and left Tina standing with us, so
Eric Watson took advantage, shimmied up close, and bawled in
Tina's ear. She responded by craning her head back and moaning
out a laugh. At that point, nothing was abnormal. An asshole
kid was getting his jollies by terrorizing a weaker creature. But
when Eric turned toward us with a proud grin, he met Joel's fist.
Surprise and welcome to humanity. I can still hear the wet sound

of Eric Watson's cheek and the thumps of his asshole body hitting each step on its way to the cement.

And so there it was. It didn't matter that Joel was defending the honor of Tina Underwood, or that she couldn't defend her defender. And it didn't matter that Joel's fist was Eric Watson's first lesson in scruples. What did matter was the open violence on the Lord's front steps.

The muffled thumps of Eric Watson's body, the silence surrounding it, the waves of knowing that push outward from such acts—whatever that is and however it works—made everyone inside the church rush out, and we all watched Mrs. Watson scurry down and gather up her wrecked son. She looked up and heaved the heaviest words she could find at Joel. "You Krugs. Just awful."

Some of us tried to explain, but we were just kids. There was too much evidence, an asshole on the ground and a bunch of Krug history. In short, Eric Watson was at church the next week and Joel wasn't. Instead, he was holed up in the shack where he'd be until Dale tried to kill him the following spring. I wouldn't see Joel, not even a hint of him, for nearly three years.

~

Without Joel, I flailed and wandered. I skipped as much school as not, and I tinkered with leaving altogether—walking off in one direction until the world ended. Some nights I stayed in the fields until the cold settled into my bones and my eyes adjusted to the slightest flickers of light. The skunks, foxes, coons, and owls got used to me. Whatever else walked around in those fields did as well. I heard sounds and songs that I've yet to understand. The dark is the dark, and I suspect it always will be.

One evening I ended up at the Peterson farm. I knew of the place, the buildings and the name, but not the life inside. I was on the far side of the road when a German shepherd came huffing down the hill. I shifted into diplomacy. "Hey there, buddy. We're buddies, right ol' buddy?" I knew the trick well enough. So I was talking fast, and that's when Helen Peterson opened the front door and yelled. It didn't work. The dog kept doing that stiff front leg bounce, so she came down and told me that Gipper just wanted to make friends.

"He needs a lesson on how to go about it," I said.

She introduced herself and I did the same. She knew that I lived in the house with the blue roof—the one three fields over. I didn't ask how.

"You live here?" I said.

"In the house I just came from," she said.

She could tell that I didn't understand—that I was trying to calculate the odds of not crossing paths—and so she gave me a lesson in local politics. Standing there in the gravel with Gipper's nose spearing my crouch, I learned a thing or two about Blakeslee and Catholics and middleclass life. She'd been attending Montpelier schools all along. Her parents had the gumption and the money to drive her into town every day, year after year. They didn't like the idea of Blakeslee, the one-room school concept, and they didn't like our teacher, which all hit me like a hose blast. I'd never met anyone with parents so devoted to education, so inclined to manage it from the outside. Helen also explained that she was Catholic, so she'd been wrapped inside the big church—the one beyond the underpass. Since I was old enough to comprehend full sentences, I'd heard hellfire proclamations against the place and all the papists therein, but here was Helen Peterson. Although I couldn't see her feet, it didn't seem like they were singed. In fact, she seemed to me the most normal human I'd met to date. I don't recall how the talk ended, but I remember her general invitation to return, which I took seriously.

By my third or fourth visit, Gipper had stopped his warning barks. I'd ask, "Where's Helen?" and he'd run ahead toward the house or barn. I'd help her lift, stack, feed, fork, and spread whatever needed it. And I listened to her say things about farming, history, food, trees, and bugs. Helen was smart. She knew things and I was glad to listen. She told me how mayflies pop out of larva stage, find a mate, copulate, grow old and die all in one day, which made me nervous for years afterward as it convinced me that some grander species watches us get born, flap around, and die in the blink of some giant eye, which was how Helen made me think in general. She showed me how to pick up a frog so it won't pee in your hand and then how to make a frog pee. She also showed me how to smoke. We were sitting with our backs against the barn, watching grasshoppers shoot like popcorn, when she pulled a cigarette from the front pocket of her coveralls and held it butt-end up. "Okay," I said. "Let me try," which was a confession. She put it in her mouth and pulled out another. She lit the match and ran it across until both were glowing. I coughed my way through mine while she smoked hers and looked at the field.

"You have brothers and sisters?" she asked.

"I had a sister," I said.

"I have a sister down in Bryan," she said. "We had a brother."

I asked for more. She told me about Jake and how he'd asphyxiated up in the silo. "He didn't come down," she said, "so Dad finally went up and found him."

I'd heard of such things. I didn't understand the chemistry of it, but I didn't have the heart to probe, so we stayed quiet and watched the grasshoppers fling themselves into the sunlight.

~

I started high school in Montpelier. That's how it worked for most of us gangly farm kids—the one-roomer in Blakeslee and then off to Montpelier or Edon, whichever was closest. I'd always disliked school, but Montpelier scraped against me like a sharp rock. It peeled me off in layers and I counted the days to when I could quit. Every time a bell rang, I saluted the hour behind me. Once, I dumped my English workbook in a toilet and then took a full-bladder whiz. I don't know why, but good riddance anyway. As far as I could tell, Montpelier High was a tomb full of worms—all but for Helen. She was a senior, older and less anxious. She'd bust out of her orbit sometimes, come around to my realm, and make sure I was okay, which I mostly wasn't.

My mother wanted me to join a sport, but I couldn't imagine myself on a football team or near a basketball court, mired in voluntary obedience. The stench of varnish and free weights, the huffy posturing—it all gave me the willies. Instead, I took up guitar. Given my situation—surrounded by corn, soybeans, and relentless quiet—guitar was either inevitable or outlandish or both.

It was an old Gretsch acoustic, a wooden tank that had been buried in my cousin's basement. When I emerged holding the thing, my mother had a look of dread. Holy Jesus, save him from his will. Of course, Jesus didn't give a damn either way, and so off I went. My cousin told me to give the Gretsch a proper home and I did. For Christmas, I got a chord book and a hymnal wrapped together—my parents' attempt to fuse the Lord Thy God and my new instrument. They insisted that I flip through it, that I try learning all the standards—How Great Thou Art, Go Tell It on the Mountain, and the like. But they knew better. By design, guitar chafed against the decorum of worship. It required too much movement, too much physical force. For Nazarenes, rigidity was the goal—the posture of consternation and worry.

Up in my room, with the door closed, I worked at mimicking the sounds quacking out of my radio. I chased after the musical stuff that I was forbidden to imagine. "Don't even think of that music," my mother once told me. But I did. Like all kids back then, I let that luscious new sound fill up all the space between thoughts. And then I started learning it one note at a time.

The fingerboard work was clenched. I twisted my left arm and wrist in various ways to allow the fingers maximum force, and sometimes I had to contort my body to get the pinky right. The nickel created ruts in my fingertips, made calluses and then tore them away, but I kept squeezing and pressing, squeezing and pressing, so by the end of the winter, I could order my fingers into the correct positions and pound out a buzzy noise. By late spring, I could stumble along with Duane Eddy. I'd follow changes or just trail behind the vocal line on one string. At some point, I figured out the standard rock-n-roll riff—the main ingredient for most every upbeat song back then—Hound Dog, Blue Suede Shoes, Red River Rock, and all the others. My mother acknowledged the progress with a declaration. "That music puts your heart out of sync with God." That was her argument. She said it softly and often. But it was the opening riff to Wake Up Little Susie that finally made her swing open my door and proclaim, "I do not approve!" I suspect she didn't know the song itself, anything about accidentally sleeping over with Susie, but the riff had a darkness—short, pentatonic, and stern. Nothing about it matched the old church hymns. Her ear could detect the rupture. She knew. Rock-n-roll guitar peeled itself away from the sonorous background of praise music, stepped to the foreground, and announced, "I am the end of civilization." And if you had ears with which to hear, you could damned well hear it. Yea verily.

~

Somehow, I maneuvered through a second year of high school. The summer after, I turned sixteen, picked up a midnight blue Chevy for fifty-five bucks, and entered moving life. I'd heard that a furniture store in Bryan was hiring fulltime warehouse guys and that age didn't matter, which was false.

"Gotta be eighteen," the guy said.

"I am," I told him.

"I am," he said in a flitty high voice, so I drove away. But fortune smiled on me anyway. In crisscrossing the streets of Bryan, I noticed a Driver Wanted sign outside Benner's Dairy. The old guy in the office, Frank Worley—or Wormly or Wurlitzer—had a stick up his butt at first. "Too young," he said. But I explained that I'd logged a good number of hours in a tractor seat as a boy, that I'd been driving big equipment around for most of my life, and he took my number. Two days later, he called and told me that milk doesn't deliver itself. The next morning, I got a ten-minute lesson on the truck—mostly about all the doors and racks—and a simple edict on community relations. "Don't bother anyone," he said. "Just drop off the order, grab the empties, and move on."

And so at sixteen, I was suddenly in charge of people's milk. You'd think I'd have learned a thing or two about trucks or deliveries or refrigeration, but I didn't. I mostly traveled the rim of Bryan and let the radio crackle out whatever could be grabbed from the air. There were plenty of dead zones, places where the music couldn't congeal and find its way down the antenna. We were in a vast plain sixty miles west of Toledo, sixty miles north-east of Ft. Wayne, and at least that far from the radio towers of Detroit. Sometimes, everything from all those cities rained down clean and easy. There was solid music on four or five spots across the dial. But usually, the songs came in intermittent waves, a chorus here, a verse there, much of it washed in static. I didn't care or know better.

On one of those mornings, I was grabbing empties by a garage door when the lead part in Blue Suede Shoes came blaring from an open kitchen window. I stayed until it stopped, dropped the tray, grabbed the empties, and drove off. I thought about it for days. I pictured Elvis's guitar player living on Route 2—hiding in a small corner of the flatland and rehearsing for a big show. Later that week, I heard it again. This time, I fidgeted with the bottles and listened through a whole song. When it stopped, I found myself standing there like an ape, waiting, looking in the window. I may have even cupped my hands against the screen. Well, I probably did. And when the sheer pulled away, I saw a face looking back at me, which is how I met Billy Rowan.

I forget how I asked, but it may have been something as flat and thoughtless as "What's going on in there?" Or maybe I complimented the guitar work. Whatever I said started a conversation about chords and lead parts—and that led to me standing in Billy's house looking at a black and white Danelectro with two lipstick pickups connected to a blond Fender amp. It was the first electric guitar I'd seen outside of television. Billy strapped it on, cranked up the volume, and let it fill the house with the same honk that I'd heard every day on the airwaves. He'd recreated the invisible—an inverse magic trick. Before I left, he invited me to bring down my old Gretsch, which I did immediately and then often. By the end of summer, I could play the twelve bar shuffle with no pauses or gaps. I learned to keep my foot pounding and align strums to the downbeat. I learned how time works, how the numbers keep repeating, how everything comes back around—how all things in the whole goddamned world come back at you again and again.

When fall came again, I let school start without me. At home each morning, I acted like I was getting up and driving into Montpelier. It was an okay charade, but I couldn't keep it going. There were too many stories to juggle, too many questions and contradictions. Or maybe I just felt wrong about it. Maybe Pastor Booth's sermons about suffering under thine iniquities had sunk in at some point. One night I got honest. "I'm done at the high school," I said.

"Done with what?" my mother said.

"Everything," I told her.

My father asked if I was quitting.

"Already did," I said.

He threw his fork down, which was more emotion than he'd shown in sixteen years. My mother threw every condemnation and warning she could muster. "Milk delivery!" she kept saying—as if milk were some transgression, as if she expected me to bloom from that dingy life into something wild and wonderful. If she did, if my father did, I never knew, but the following week I decided to ruin my life officially by moving out. I'd already stopped attending church and going to school. I'd forsaken Jesus, formal education, and everything else. I was kite with a broken string.

Billy offered me a spare room where I piled up blankets and made a nest on the floor. With that, I was living on the rim of a town ten times the size of Blakeslee, even bigger than Montpelier, brimming with all kinds of trouble.

The first night, I paced around the square for hours, marveling at the giant bricks in the courthouse and all the movement spinning around me. If I'm honest, and I have no reason to be otherwise, Bryan was a beacon. Helen had graduated, held off on college for some reason I never gleaned, and moved down to live with her older sister. She'd been there since June working at the library, and that made Bryan feel like the next step in evolution, the place a human would go to lose gills and start breathing air. I don't suppose that's biologically correct, but it's true. All the Helens of the world moved to Bryan and all the people like me followed.

A few days after getting settled, I mustered up my juices and walked through the heavy glass doors of the library. There she was, standing on one of those mini ladders and re-shelving books. Inside of a few seconds, she put everything together because that's what her brain did.

"Done with school already?"

"Not really," I said. "I let it start without me."

She didn't laugh, and I felt a kick in the gut. My parents could have pulled my skin off and it wouldn't have registered, but Helen's look of disapproval made me want to drive back to Montpelier and beg to start my junior year. I didn't, of course.

She gave me the library tour—pointing to the sections and explaining the shelving process as though I were a civilized community member. I followed her and imagined myself coming back, checking out all the novels I'd skimmed or skipped along the way. And then back in a small corridor, stowed away among oversized books, she ended the tour. "So that's it," she said. "Other than quitting school, what are you up to?"

Her question felt like an invitation. We'd never flirted or even danced around intimacy. In a way, Helen was all business. She established the nature of things and everyone else got in line. I did anyway. But on that particular day, squeezed up close and surrounded by bookshelves, she seemed less solid, less direct. It could have been the situation—both of us in our new lives, nothing of the old forces around us. I looked, maybe for the first time, straight into both eyes and stared without blinking at her perfect mouth. And she responded by standing a little straighter, pulling her shoulders back a hint, showing me what I already understood about her structure.

I didn't know what to say or how to manage the quiet stuff fluttering in the air. The only thing I could conjure was my burgeoning musical enterprise. I explained it all—how I'd learned some guitar and how I was living with Billy on Route 2. Next to me quitting school and the formality of the library, the news had sizzle. Helen lit up about it. She asked when she'd get to hear us play.

"Pretty soon," I said.

"Well, I hope so," she said.

And I walked out of there with blurred vision.

~

Billy said it was time to go electric. And that made sense because my fingers were red and torn up. I'd been banging that Gretsch like a drum, doing everything possible to keep up with wattage. I'd pulled together forty bucks and we drove into Flannery's, the only place in the county that carried electric guitars. If you wanted something with wires and couldn't drive to Toledo or Ft. Wayne, you had to deal with Flannery—the smell of farts, halitosis, and burnished brass. When we entered, Flannery stayed perched behind his counter and looked over the top of his glasses. We stood facing him for several seconds, longer than anyone should have to stand in front of anyone else in silence, before he asked if we needed something specific. He made me say exactly what I wanted—name and model number.

"You want to buy or just fiddle with it?"

"Buy," I said.

He sighed, put his pork-colored arms on the counter, and said the Danelectros were fifty bucks plus tax. He didn't have any in stock. If I wanted one, he needed half down.

I tried to say something shrewd. "Will that guarantee I get one when they come in?"

"Well," he said, looking at Billy—not me, "if you can pay the balance when the guitar comes in, you'll get one." He said it like a punchline. He was that kind of asshole. And truth be told, I almost hurled something at him. I could feel a tingly energy crawling up my spine, telling me to grab a ukulele from the wall and make that geezer eat it.

Billy had the brains to yank me toward the door where we were free to think. I wanted to walk out or at least act like it, but Flannery halted things.

"I got something else back here," he said. Then he came out with a silversparkle, two pickup Silvertone. "I got it in yesterday. It's used but clean."

He plugged it in and handed it over. I turned up all the knobs and played a few rhythms while they looked on. I could hardly keep my wits, so I passed it to Billy. He played in the back pickup, then popped it into that single-coil throaty sound. The speaker on the amp huffed a little with the low notes and exhaled to a stop with Billy's last chord. "That's a winner," he said.

"Forty bucks, forty-five with a soft case," Flannery said.

A few minutes later, I was walking out with sunlight twinkling on the sparkle finish. It was the most exotic thing I'd ever seen anywhere. Surrounded by the Bryan streets, it may as well have been a unicorn, and for all the reasons in the world of men and women, boys and girls, I wanted Helen to marvel along with me. When I walked into the library and saw Helen's eyes pop, my blood carbonated.

Out at Billy's, we plugged both guitars into the Fender. Billy tweaked up the volume, counted off, and we created a chordal stampede, all twelve strings vying for airspace, which is why we didn't hear the front door open or Billy's neighbor from across Route 2 bawling us out. At some point, I caught his arms flailing in my periphery, stopped, and heard "no more of this awful shit crap! I won't have it! That's all! I'm done! And if you don't believe me, just play one more sonofabitchin note!" That's how it went. No more of this awful shit crap, etc. It was the first bawl-out but not the first conflict. Apparently, this guy had already called the police a few times, and they told Billy, in that mysterious police language, that they were done warning him, which made him assume they'd come out with some head-thunking tool designed just for guitar players. It was a new a new kind of criminality, so the cops were probably ad libbing, but Billy wasn't taking chances. He went out the door, crossed the road, and tried to patch things up. A few minutes later, he walked in and made the official announcement: "No more guitar on Route 2."

~

With the neighbor problem hanging, we set out to build a band. Billy drove us into town to meet up with Eddie Wilson, who played drums and lived in his mother's basement. The whole thing took a few minutes. Billy knocked once and Eddie came to the door. He took us straight to the basement and showed us his powder blue Ludwig set crammed between the washer and furnace.

"They look great," I said.

"Sound great too," he said.

"Can you give us a little demonstration?" Billy asked.

"Not with Mom home," Eddie said.

"Well, we need a drummer," Billy said.

"You got one," Eddie said.

Eddie was as close to a leprechaun—complete with floppy red hair—as a grown man can be. He was short but sharp. That's how I thought of him. Most people missed his shrewdness because he talked from the middle of his mouth, which meant a few important sounds went missing. He tried extra hard to be friendly and usually pulled it off. Other than being called a leprechaun now and then, Eddie lived easily down there in his own layer. And from the first meeting, I liked him. Before we played together or practiced or anything, the three of us decided we'd be a band. We only needed a place to work at full volume, and Eddie had the answer—a pal of his just north of West Unity who'd just inherited his parents' farmhouse.

When the three of us pulled into Lance Delaney's driveway, I felt like it wouldn't work. The house looked like a museum—a relic from the 1800s, obstinate, quiet, flipping the bird at the twentieth century. Eddie introduced us in the front yard and asked straightaway before we'd even gotten past the niceties if we could invade. "Hey, Lant. Can we practik in your livingroom?"

Lance looked at us and nodded. He wasn't all that tall, but he had a television cowboy thing going—a controlled comfort, like he'd grown accustom to letting things roll up to him. He enjoyed the request, mulling it over in front of us, and then agreeing. "Well," he said, "I don't see why that wouldn't be an adventure."

We drove back to town, got the amp, the guitars, and Eddie's drums. That evening, we played our first song—one of those guitar zingers by Duane Eddie. The livingroom had hardwood floors, giant arching windows, and a high coved ceiling—architecture built for dynamiting sound. Overtones shot in every direction so that every molecule was bonked and saturated. We watched Eddie for the last cymbal crash and tried not to look surprised that we'd created such bombast. Behind his own giddiness, Billy said, "That was pretty good." We then hammered through several renditions of every song we could conjure—one after the other and then all of them again.

Lance called a meeting, got us beers, lit a cigarette, and paced. He asked if we'd be ready for the public in two weeks. We said yes, of course, and Lance explained that his house would be the sight of the biggest party ever, that we'd drive out all the ghosts and sadness for miles around.

~

That week, I almost ran over Joel. He was walking on Route 34, just north of Bryan. I passed him, looked in my right mirror, which had nearly clipped his shoulder, and thought I was looking at Dale Krug. I kept looking, swerved into the gravel, and went another half mile or so to the next stop. I exchanged the crate and watched the road. Maybe I expected Dale to come staggering along—finally forced into a pedestrian life. When he got close enough to make out, I knew. We both knew. Three years had passed. But Joel and I recognized each other's posture and whatever vibrations make people distinguishable from others. He was taller, skinnier, like he'd been stretched, and the stretching brought out an unmistakable Daleness. The genetic stuff swimming around in Joel's blood had done its work. He was Dale's progeny, no getting around it. They had the same angles and cuts, the same tight neck. You could see every word being made or swallowed. But Dale leaned forward at the world like an upright gargoyle. Without that lean, Joel's edges worked. He was a handsome kid.

We stood on the berm talking a mile a minute, and we laughed at the last thing we'd witnessed—Eric Watson tumbling down the Nazarene steps, his mother, all puckered and sour-mouthed, prying him from the concrete, the whole congregation standing in haughty righteousness. I told Joel how I quit being a Nazarene a few weeks later, right after Eric Watson tried to goad me into a brawl.

"You sock him in the other cheek?" he asked.

I wished like crazy that I had.

With cars zooming by us, he nutshelled the last few years of his life—how he'd freed himself from Dale two years prior, that he walked away from the little shack one night and never went back. Since then, he'd been living and working at the Sholwalter farm between Bryan and Montpelier. As the hired hand, he was charged with all the labor—feeding the animals, cleaning shit, maintaining equipment, everything really. I'm not sure about his wages, but I know he was given a handful of cash at the end of each week, so he'd been doing pretty well. He seemed pumped and ready for anything. As for why he was walking up the road, his Plymouth, which he'd just bought, had sputtered out.

I drove him back to the Sholwalter farm and told him how I'd learned guitar, how I met Billy, Eddie, and Lance, and that we were planning a huge party over in West Unity.

"Can I come?" he asked.

"You'll be the goddamned guest of honor," I told him.

And so Joel and I were back. Just like that. He came to our next rehearsal and sat on the sofa shaking his head—awed, I guess, at everything, where we were, what I was doing, what it all felt like in the moment.

That night, we sat by a fire—Joel, Eddie, Billy, Lance, and I all hyped and rumbling with wolfpack muster. The empty bottles formed a ring around us. The dark came in close and we conjured visions of a rambunctious future. We saw ourselves loose and uncontained, like vapor, like some blurry thing not yet invented, and for some reason, we talked Joel into leaving school, which he hadn't done yet. The Sholwalters wanted him to keep attending, at least most days. That was part of the deal: he could live there and earn a little as long as he stayed in school. But the big craven world was waiting. That was our point.

"Jut walk out," Eddie said. "Jut walk out." He kept saying it and then demonstrated for us, marching away from the circle of light.

Lance argued that school didn't matter anymore. "That era's over," he said. And he didn't mean it personally—like it was over for Joel. He meant it historically. He was convinced that schools were a thing of the past, that people were on the cusp of cutting the cord to all such stuff, that humanity was ready to take learning back into itself, away from buildings and chalkboards and those mean little desks. That's how Lance thought. And it was hard to doubt him.

Billy tried to balance things out. He said, well, you know, it's not all bad and so on, but he was one moderate voice in a yard of sweaty hooligans. Everything that mattered was begging us to fling ourselves into it. What in holy hell did school have to do with anything? Why would someone who could choose otherwise keep on sitting in those desks, those sticky wooden torture boxes, and suck down all those rules? What's the point? I asked that and plenty more until halfway through a beer, Joel raised his bottle and announced his official separation from all formal education and its mounds of steaming bullshit. I thereby witnessed and conferred upon him the freedom he hath deserved. Someone said, "Amen." And I said, "yea verily."

~

Before the party—a week or so out—Lance and Joel decided to rip out the main banister so people could sit on the steps and let their legs dangle. It took a few minutes from decision to an open stairway. There was sawing and kicking and then a celebration of open space. And with that accomplished, Lance sawed a window in the wall so people could stand in the diningroom and see through. Billy tried to stop him, but that wall was a goner. We stood there and watched the saw poking through, ramming in and out of the old cakey plaster, and then Lance's fist pop into the livingroom like Lazarus's hand from the tomb.

That night or the next or the one before—I don't recall because it's all smashed together—Joel decided that we needed a name. Over a regime of beers and a bottle of Wild Irish Rose, we conjured a list of mostly offensive phrases. I recall a few of the more serious candidates: The Three Muskateers, The Hotrods, The Amps, Billy and the Goats, The Unsettlers, and The Disappearing Kids. Joel suggested the Goddamn Hammerhead Kids— Dale Krug's pet name for his brood. We chewed on that and alternative versions, the Hammerhead Kids or the Hammerheads, but Billy said people would think of sharks, beaches, the Beach Boys, and that heap of silliness. We agreed on The Amps. It sounded electric, sizzling, full of the future. We said a bunch of yea verilies and it was official.

I should say this. The Bible talk was my doing. I didn't know it at the time, but I was discovering a drive to stomp out the past—to beat it or kick it around in some fashion. I hated the sound of it, the language, anything that rang of family, relatives, the places we gathered, the lives we'd been forced to lead because of lineage and nothing else. Ever since my uncle grabbed me in the barn and mostly got what he wanted, I was geared up to smash my way out. I was seven at the time, and I didn't acknowledge or comprehend it for decades. My uncle blew his head off with a shotgun not long after the incident in the barn, but that hadn't helped or hurt me. I was left to brood on my own. And there was something in these days with Lance, Joel, Eddie, and Billy that torqued me up, something that forced me toward the next phase, whatever it was. Plus, there was my little sister who'd died before she could even talk. The past was a mammoth hand pressing down. I hated every minute behind me and every second that wasn't now.

~

A few days before the party, I pulled up to the library, left the Benner truck idling, and ran inside. I'd written down directions, and even drew a little map so Helen could find her way. I walked past a room of kids sitting on the floor—all crossed legged and attentive in the half-dark. They were listening to a woman read in dramatic tones. She was whooping and whispering and pronouncing everything hard. And that scene, or maybe the way a few kids turned and looked when they heard my shoes scraping in the main corridor, announced the reality of Helen's life. She was a real librarian. She worked in a formal building with formal affairs. I thought of Lance's livingroom, all slashed and kicked open, the yard where Lance promised he'd someday do a firewalk, and the mound of beer bottles that had accumulated over the weeks. I wanted to turn around and let Helen have her own life. It would've been better that way. But she looked up, waved me over, and we talked by the magazine rack. I handed her the directions because there they were—an obvious sheet of paper in the air between us. She said she'd come, no doubt about it.

~

We showed up in the afternoon. Lance had emptied the house, gutted it so that every surface of the first floor was clean and ready for feet, butts, or drinks. He'd cleared his refrigerator of everything but beer and pink wine. He positioned hard liquors on the counter with all the labels facing out. "Jesus Harold Christ," he said. "We're gonna peel off the paint." Even Billy, who'd been around and seen some parties, was awed at the possibility. I stood in the diningroom looking through the sawed-out window, which had been widened and lengthened so that it was nearly another door, and I imagined what people would do, how they'd stand, how they'd react when hit with the music.

By evening, the crowd started pulling in. Lance met cars at the end of the driveway and directed them to the side lawn. The early arrivals were Lance's friends and neighbors. There was Sarah Shirky, Lance's girlfriend and eventual wife. She talked loud and spouted profanities. She'd call you a cunt or prick with no compunction, but she also enjoyed people. If someone had a story, she'd be the first in line—right up front, holding her breath at all the important parts, hollering out "whoooo-boy" at the climax and cursing in sympathy. She was easy to like. There was also Sheila and Stacey Kloster, who lived a mile down the road. They were different eggs from the same nest. Sheila was thick and quiet, Stacey thin and cranked up. And there was Peckerhead Phil, who was taller than Lance, taller than two full Eddies.

When Lance introduced him—"Everyone, introducing Sir Peckerhead Phil!"—Phil socked him in the shoulder. He resented it,
but everyone called him Peckerhead Phil anyway. He had a neck
the length of most people's forearms. His head didn't resemble
anything in particular, but it sat atop that spindly neck. He was
generally quiet and seemed content up above the madding crowd.
And there was Toad Bissell, who knew things, and most of what
he said seemed accurate, like he'd actually read it somewhere.
Toad's presence allowed us to wonder aloud why crops spurt up
at night, not during the day, why beer makes people loud and
liquor makes people hate themselves, why the Indians lost, how
people decided on state capitals, why the oceans contain salt, how
rivers decide which way to flow, what creates the northern lights,
why people don't dream of being dead.

And then came the Russians, Nicholas and Eva, the oldest
of the group. During the war, they'd been nabbed by Germans
and stashed in a camp. At the time, they were children, but I
suspect they collected a good number of scenes that imaginations
can't conjure without help. Eva had little to say about that time,
but Nicholas would reveal things. He'd explain the regularity of
it—sleeping, cleaning, eating in the late morning. Their camp
was won and opened by the Americans just before the war ended.
After months of wandering around in Russia and looking for
their town beneath the rubble, their relatives decided to leave
the continent behind. In America, Nicholas and Eva grew up
together and then married. They were a conclave of memory.
They carried a balled-up past, details of their rural homeland, the
horrors of the camp, and the struggle to grow up here. And now
they were working and living on a big poultry farm down the
road from Lance. They were, like the rest of us, living that horizontal life—roaming and forgetting, roaming and forgetting.

And I'll say this because it's true. We were a cloud of trouble. There's no getting around it. We were a swirl of doom, and I was at the middle of it.

At the start, everyone huddled in the kitchen. They took turns watching through the hole. I suspect it was too loud—louder than the body wants—but after a few songs, Lance started pulling people into the livingroom. Literally, he started yanking and pushing. And I remember the Kloster sisters standing in front of us, petrified, wincing, and pinned against the wall. At the end of the song, they clapped politely, and an hour later—somehow— the room was full and sweaty and roaring. Just like that. Toad was standing between Billy and me—his eyes closed, his head down and his body gyrating. The Kloster sisters were whirling. Peckerhead Phil was bobbing among Sarah's friends. Sarah was bent over and pounding her feet into the floor like she was killing bugs. Nicholas was facing the wall and banging both hands against the plaster with every downbeat. Eva stood beside him yelling something into the air, something serious, maybe curative.

We took a break, so I wormed through a gauntlet of backslaps and freed myself into the night air. Lance's yard had been populated. Clumps of onlookers had formed around the windows. It seemed like the whole area—everyone who wasn't tied down or sealed up—had been pulled away from their lives and sucked into Lance's yard. I made my way to the rim of light and tried counting the cars strung bumper to bumper on both sides, the chrome winking from twenty, fifty, a hundred yards in both directions. It was true. Everything Lance said was true. It was the biggest party ever, all the sadness gone, the ghosts flung to far corners. But here's the important part—the part that changed everything. When I came back into the light, I saw a circle of lawn chairs. All but two were empty. Helen and Joel had found one another.

It's hard for me to see this from anyplace other than where I am, but I must have felt something—some resignation or sense that I'd fulfilled my purpose. I don't know exactly. I felt other things as well, dark forces, but they were muted by the rush of the whole night and the months before it. In that blink of time, everything felt like everything else.

After another long set of music, hours of noise, pounding, and arms stretched at the ceiling, Lance made a bonfire in the yard and we circled around the flames. At the end, it was just us mongrels who didn't have to be home—or who had decided that home didn't matter anymore. Helen and Joel sat wrapped in one another.

"You two gonna git married?" Eddie asked.

They smiled and let someone else answer.

"A Nazarene and a Catholic!"

"Do they allow that?"

"Not in Blakeslee," Joel said.

I sat on a log, drank fast, and let my thoughts twirl into the autumn sky. I felt volcanic. I told everyone how Joel had knocked Eric Watson silly on the steps of the Nazarene church and how I thought rock-n-roll had come along to knock all the Eric Watsons in the goddamned face. Lance took off his shirt and ran laps around the house, and then I explained how Kathryn Mueller, the only Nazarene girl back up in Blakeslee who had any life to her, could fly. I told them how Joel and I believed it, that it was true, that anyone who doubted was a complete lunatic, and I remember that Helen jumped in and explained how they found Kathryn Mueller dead in a field.

"What's that prove?" Toad asked.

And so Joel and I explained it all—how we'd talked to Kathryn Mueller after church when we were young but not so young to be swayed by bullshit. And we explained how nobody ever found footprints in the field, how they found Kathryn one morning, just her flattened body smashed into the mud, and how the people at church whispered or prayed about it. As Joel and I talked, everyone else went silent. They listened and let us weave together bits of memory. And then Joel yelled at the sky and asked Kathryn, straight to her face, how she did it.

"Hey, Kathryn!!" he said.

We all looked up. Everyone did.

"Hey, Kathryn! How'd you do it?"

She didn't answer, and it didn't matter.

I woke up to the sun scratching at my eyelid. I don't know who drove away, who passed out on the ground, who made their way to cars or Lance's floor. Helen and Joel had veered off together in some quiet moment, in one of those collective blinks when everyone chases an idea through their own minds or across the sky.

~

"I want in." Those were Joel's first words after the party. He wanted into the music.

I asked him what he wanted to do. He didn't know exactly. I asked if he could sing, but he'd mostly just talked his whole life. That's how he put it.

"We need a singer," I told him.

"What about another guitar player? You could teach me."

"Three guitars?"

"I don't know. Why not? If two, why not three?"

He was fixated on the idea, but I was curious about Helen—how they'd managed to strike up a conversation, how he'd done what I'd failed to do in my sixteen and a half years, how he'd landed a girl, especially a girl like Helen.

"What about Helen?" I asked.

"What about her?"

"What do you think?"

"I think she's a queen." That's what he said. I wished I'd invented the idea, but I didn't. And looking back, I know why Joel wanted into the music, why he wanted it to come from his own body. The music was a new place beyond us. It catapulted all possibilities up and out—into some electric nowhere.

Joel and I got into a routine. Both of us had morning jobs—his getting food to livestock, mine getting milk to humans—but by noon, he'd come running up Billy's steps and wait at the door. I got accustomed to seeing his face through the screen. "What's the plan?" he'd say. There was no plan, but we'd meander and talk music until we'd wrapped every song we knew in some theoretical concoction: Johnny and the Hurricanes, more than anyone else who tried, had found the right formula for resuscitating classics. Carl Perkins had the perfect vocal tone for rock ensemble, and Pat Boone was rock-n-roll's greatest enemy—the frequencies in his voice lining up in utter contradiction to the sonic allure of electric guitar. On one of those afternoons, Joel yelled, "Fuck Pat Boone! Fuck that guy!" over and over out the passenger window. I drove and he yelled his head off. It was one of those moments when you know what's true.

Meanwhile, Billy had been planning the next phase. One night in Lance's kitchen, he laid out the future: First, someone had to start singing. We all knew it, but Billy was adamant. He was against freestanding singers—one guy in front with nothing but a microphone. "They suck up all the energy," he said. Second, we needed a bass player. Third, we needed to go public, and that was the most obvious. The party had put us in motion. All the convulsing in Lance's livingroom was a contract, an official deal between us and everyone else: we'd play, they'd love it.

Joel wanted to talk about bass. "How hard is it?"

"It depends on the song," Billy said.

"Hard as guitar?"

"Not really. There are only four strings and you don't play chords."

Joel looked over and grinned his plan at me.

The next day, we were in Flannery's studying two basses on the wall—a Fender Precision and a Harmony. Flannery came around from his perch, rolled an amp toward us, plugged in the Harmony—probably because he knew the Fender was too much—and handed it over. Joel plucked the open strings and let them bloat out until the snare drums on the opposite wall sounded like rain.

"Cool," he said. "How much?"

"Seventy," Flannery said.

Joel looked at me. I had no idea. Neither of us were experienced enough to make distinctions. We could enjoy the shapes, colors, and the big sounds coming from the amp, but that was all. It was the dumb leading the innocent. For any commitments, we needed Billy.

"Any chance you'll have some more options soon?" Joel asked.

"What you looking for?"

"Not sure yet," Joel said. "I just want to see what's out there."

Flannery looked like he might puke. He wanted a quick deal, payment for something already hanging on the walls, not a long-term relationship with an unhinged teenager.

"I never know what's coming," he said. "I could get a used one in tomorrow or next month."

"We'll be back," I told him.

So we came out empty handed, but the trip to Flannery's formalized the idea. Joel was bound for bass. Out at Billy's, I got him familiar with a fingerboard on my old Gretsch. I explained the geography and told him to worry about the first four strings. "They're the same as bass," I said. "No difference."

"But those seemed a hell of a lot bigger."

"The notes are the same," I told him.

"How's that possible?" he said.

Joel was no dummy. I explained best I could how octaves work, how an F is an F regardless, and how the notes walk up to the fifth fret and then start again on the next string.

He asked why there was no B sharp.

"Just one of those things," I said. "No E sharp, no B sharp."

"Why not? What'd they do wrong?"

"Stopped going to church," I said.

"Good for them," he said.

~

When Lance broke the news about the racetrack gig, he seemed like a proud father. We were circled at the table. "My lady," he said, "has engineered your second show at Polk's."

He was talking about Polk's Raceway—a track, grandstand, and country music stronghold. After Saturday races, people would come for square dances and cold bottled beer. But in the off-season, after the summer frenzy, the crowds shrank. With a wane in business on the horizon, Leonard Polk—who went by Len—was willing to try anything. When his niece, Sarah, described the droves of people who'd shown up to a house party outside of West Unity, Len was open to the possibilities.

"He'll pay thirty bucks in cash at the end of the night if it goes well." That's how Lance framed it. "We'll get word out," he said. "The place'll be mobbed."

That weekend, we piled into Lance's car and headed for the raceway. We paid fifty cents each for cover, which I thought was robbery, and walked into a huge cement room where a three-piece band was chirping through gray circular horns. The guitar and banjo players sat on stools, and the caller, who also jabbed at a fiddle, stomped on the rim of the stage. They were crammed, their elbows knocking into each other's ribs. We stayed just inside the threshold and studied it all. We tried to imagine Eddie's drums and all our bodies stuffed on that perch. It didn't help that the band looked like some of the Nazarene coots, freed from their teal plaid jackets and ties. It also didn't help that there were twenty, maybe fewer, people in the place, a handful of dancers obediently performing the allemande lefts and do-si-dos without cracking a smile.

"They look mad about it," Joel said.

"You'd be too," I told him.

"Already am," he said back.

We walked in behind Lance, and the little flock of square dancers studied us. At the bar, we stood between stools. Even though the place was huge, it felt like we'd walked into someone's house on Christmas Eve and kicked grandma in the shin.

"These guys will be playing here next month," Lance said.

The bartender, a lumbering oaf whom we came to know as Barney—Barney the Bartender—looked at him.

"Okay then," Lance said, and he ordered beers.

Joel and I passed. We stood mute. I knew what the other guys were thinking, and I was thinking the same. This couldn't possibly work. And that's when Billy told me over the top of his beer that I should try singing.

"Why me?" I said.

"I've heard you working through songs. You can do it."

"I'll have to think about it."

Billy's suggestion hadn't come out of thin air. He meditated on things. Granted, the situation—standing in that big cement cavern with square dance music chirping through the P.A.—may have forced it up sooner than expected, but the idea had been brewing.

Lance downed his beer and gave us all a look. On the way out, I noticed the "No Twisting" sign by the door.

~

Despite the cement walls and the angry square dancers, the racetrack pumped us full of muster. Having seen the place, Billy had two objectives: that I start singing and that we get Joel ready. He was adamant about both, insisting that we had to fill the whole spectrum—bass on the bottom, vocals on the top. Otherwise, it'd be a murky swath of mids.

In the privacy of the dairy truck, I tried out my voice. It felt okay, not native but not foreign either. I'd been studying all those sounds, the way singers curl their vowels, clip off some words and protract others depending on placement—verse or chorus or bridge. I'd been carrying those maneuvers around and loading them into my throat. The hard part was playing and singing—getting my mouth and body to recognize one another. Without conscious effort to marry them up, they're separate operations. I learned that much. They might have the same address but that's it. Sometimes, words ended up with an extra syllable. Other times, my arm just stopped. At rehearsal, the beat started gluing things together, creating a foundation so I could coast over the mental hiccups. I had to rely on the rhythm beneath my own thinking and loosen my grip on the guitar. Goodbye fingers, hello song. And if I look at the whole process, I think it's a big fling outward—fingers, chords, songs, audience, and then history. That's how I see my life. Not that it's important here, but after Joel disappeared, I left the flatland and got caught up in whatever current there was. Fingers, chords, songs, audience, history. That's how it goes.

Getting Joel up to speed required all hands, all wallets and wheels. We pooled money and invaded Flannery's on a Saturday afternoon. Nothing else had come in. We stood by the Harmony and talked it over. Billy tested it while Joel stood clenched.

"You want that bass?" Flannery asked.

"Maybe," Billy said. "You got an amp?"

Flannery got huffy and rolled out a little Ampeg—a thigh-high boxy thing that looked like a sewing machine. Billy nodded, turned it on, checked the tubes, and plugged in. The whole store—the whole damned block—purred from it.

Flannery wanted some crazy amount—hundreds just for the Ampeg, more for chords, more for a case, and on and on. Billy stood up and told him flat-out, "We'll go two hundred for both— bass and amp. Otherwise, we're going to Ft. Wayne."

I wanted to spice up the offer and add in a swift kick to the nuts, but Flannery accepted and even polished up the Harmony before handing it over. That night, Lance's old house vibrated to Joel's bass. The maple floors, put down at the end of another century, couldn't have imagined it. Whatever ghosts were still hanging around packed up and got the hell out.

And from there, it was boot camp for fingers and ears, nonstop work. Joel was trying, inside of a month, to understand what the rest of us had been chasing for years. Through talking, eating, drinking, he had his fingers on the neck. I remember him walking down the hall from the latrine with the bass strapped behind him. At Lance's, he'd sit in front of us, elbows on his knees, studying everything. He pointed out changes, nodded, sometimes closed his eyes and moved his fingers along with us. Afterward, he'd listen to Billy's lessons—general theories about the mechanics of music. We all listened, sometimes debating the best chord progressions, the best way to resolve things or transition to a bridge. One night, Lance got all ruffled about the theories, threw up his arms, and asked where in the living hell Billy had learned such stuff.

"It's just ensemble," Billy said.

"That's what I'm talking about," Lance said. "Where'd you get that goddamned word?"

Billy explained his years in band and orchestra—how he learned to play cello and then trumpet. Lance said it was all bullshit, that you don't learn how to play rock-n-roll from trumpets and that Billy was some kind of freak musical genius but wouldn't fucking admit it. Joel or I—one of us—said a yea verily.

~

I'm not saying we were ready for the show because we weren't. We knew progressions, fundamentals, how to make serious noise. We were relying on history—on the sheer fact that live rock and roll was novel, a new animal altogether.

When we pulled into the raceway, a black and white sign on a rusty trailer announced us: *Tonight: Rock/Roll Dance, featuring The Amps. 8:00 to 11:00.* Joel came out of his skin. We all did. We huddled outside the door, cooled our jets, and walked in. Across the cement expanse, we saw Barney standing by a rotund guy on

a stool. That guy was Len Polk. He didn't look like Sarah's uncle,
a guy you'd call Len, or a guy who'd run a racetrack. I expected
a pumped up jawbone of a dude with a high collar and slick hair.
But Len had no edges. He was an old tire. To this day, whenever
I think of being worn out, I think of Len Polk. He was exhaus-
tion incarnate. Every gesture murmured it—halfway returning
his hanky to his pocket, halfway pushing the hair across his
forehead, letting those huge glasses fall to the very edge of his
nose, and when scratching his leg, lifting his calf just far enough
to rendezvous with his hand. He even pointed by sloughing his
arm out in a general direction. Everything was calculated for
minimal effort. He used people, situations, booze, music, and all
physical matter within range to make things easier on himself.

Billy made the trek across the room while we watched from
the threshold. In the distance, we saw Len look at his watch,
back at the stage, at Barney, and then shrug. Billy came back
with the news. "Well," he said, "we can set up." And that was
something—the official go-ahead.

It took a while—fidgeting with the stage, that little perch
made for three skinny geezers and no equipment, dealing with
Barney, who seemed oddly fussy about the microphone and P.A.,
positioning the amps at the right angle, and fretting about everything from floor to ceiling. Billy asked if we could run through a
song to get a feel for the room. Barney had no sense of the question or the language that made it. "Hurryitup," he said. He was
one of those guys—and they were everywhere—who smashed
his words together, who couldn't afford the energy to insert gaps.
Joel said that the poor guy had a dead cat up his ass.

Eddie clicked off and each count snapped back at us from a distance. The music did the same. It bounced against the underbelly
of the grandstand steps and came washing back at us chewed up

and garbled. And that wasn't the worst of it. A few measures in, a low dirge swelled up from nowhere, consumed every other note, and rang out in triumph. Joel gave me a look—something like regret, like if I decided to unplug and run like a raped ape out the door, he'd be on my heels. But we stayed put and groped our way through the song. By the chorus, I aimed myself at the mic, focused my eyes on the spit screen and let loose. I heard myself splashing around in the distance, my voice lagging like in some noisy dream.

We crashed to a stop and stared at Billy. "Cement," he said. The big cavern was creating a demonic reverb. We stood around like idiots looking into the distance, at the bass amp, at the mic. Joel knew the swell had some relationship to his bass. He offered to sit it out, to let us go on without him, which no one accepted. Billy rolled off the low end on the amp and aimed it toward the bar, which made Len roll off his stool and head into a back room. We tried again. It didn't work. That same dirge came back, maybe louder than before.

Billy gave in, decided it'd be fine, that people would soak it up. We just needed bodies in the room—flesh and clothing to absorb all the low-end. I thought he was placating. I figured the whole night was fizzling away.

Lance ordered us to his car. He passed around a bottle of something strong, Thunderbird or the like, and tried to talk us up. He'd become the ringmaster, the rabblerouser—the guy who lights the cannon wick. He was working hard, but we were fixated on the bass problem and the empty parking lot. We stayed quiet and let a stiff fall wind blow against the windows.

"What if no one comes?" Eddie said.

"What if everyone comes?" Lance said.

If it's not clear already, Lance was some kind of wizard. He had a sense of what people are, what they need. And when I think about him back then—an orphaned flatlander with nothing but his parents' old house—I wonder how in the hell he gathered up so much clarity. "The problem," he told us, "won't ever be lack of people. Not in this operation, not with you guys." He was right.

At some point, we got tired of eyeballing the parking lot and went inside. We hung around the bar, tuned up for the umpteenth time. Then a few partygoers came in—Peckerhead Phil, Toad, the Kloster sisters, and Helen. They convened around a pillar a good twenty yards from the stage area.

At 8:00, Barney said we could wait another fifteen minutes. He said it like an offer, but it was more of a jab. Nothing was happening. The place was almost deserted. And in the timeless standoff between bands and bars, an empty room always discredits the band. We knew it. He knew it. We stood by the bar—Billy drinking a beer, Joel and I drinking Coke. I imagined Len sitting somewhere in the back, hands over his face, asking the air what he'd agreed to. And for some reason, the partygoers kept their distance and we kept ours.

By 8:30, we counted twenty-three people. Barney gave us a nod and leaned on the bar. "We normally go three sets," he said. "You play for forty-five, take a break, forty-five, another break, and then finish out the night. Okay. Better hit it."

And so there it was, the marching order from Barney the Bartender. All twenty-three people—in small clumps—watched us head for our instruments. I remember strapping on the Silvertone and being damned glad that it covered my midsection.

Like in warm-up, Eddie clicked off and the sound blasted out like a train in a cyclone. I wanted to apologize to everyone for coming out, for spending money to get in, for getting all revved up. The bass dirge came along about halfway through the song, dipped away, and then returned as a full roar that lasted a good twenty seconds after us. When it dissipated, a few people applauded.

We started another song. I didn't sing. I couldn't bring myself to approach the mic, to throw another sound into the swirl. Instead, I kept my head down and my eyes on the fingerboard—convinced that I'd never mount a stage again. We gnashed our teeth, the Book of Revelations hard at work, and hammered through each song on the little list Billy had written. Finally, I announced that we'd be back in fifteen minutes—mostly as an apology.

Lance came running up and ordered us to his car again. We all went—Billy, Eddie, Joel, Helen, Sarah, and I all passing the bottle, breathing hard, and listening to Lance's sermon. "They love it," he said. "They're fixed on you guys. Everyone's watching." I didn't accept it. I knew what it sounded like—the garbled noise and strange moans. And I could see the rigid bodies. Whenever I allowed myself a glance, I saw nothing but still life.

And that's when Helen broke in. She had a theory. It was the big cement cavern. The size of it intimidated everyone, not like Lance's livingroom, which felt like a secret huddle. Of course, she was right. The beauty of Lance's party was bound up in that old house, its walls like a cradle against the nonstop horizon.

Sarah piped up. She'd counted fifty-one people come in through the first set—which meant Len had already covered expenses. "He's thrilled," she said.

"Jeremy," Lance said, fully turned around with his butt on the steering wheel, honking for effect, "It's up to you. No one knows what to do. They're waiting for you to tell them."

"I can't make the place any smaller," I told him.

"Make it feel smaller. Say stuff. Use the mic that God hath given."

I wanted to know what to say. He said anything—any god-damned thing in the world. "Tell them you like ice cream! Tell them you like beer—or beer and ice cream. They need to hear that it's okay. They need a human voice." And that made good sense.

When we went back in, the place looked full—alive and ready. I hadn't taken stock during the first set, but they were right. Even though most of the room was empty, the mass of bodies around the bar and toward the stage mattered.

I geared up, went to the mic, and yelled out the name of the first song, Flying Saucer Rock-n-Roll. Lance and Sarah met in the center—where square dancers had been *do-si-do*-ing for years—and started a big open-arm twist. Helen and the Kloster sisters jumped in with them. Then the clump at the bar flowed in as well—Peckerhead Phil drifting like a cut buoy toward the middle. A song later, all the clumps had congealed. We were either ignoring the echoes or the crowd had chased them into the ceiling. After Good Golly Miss Molly, which I sang like a timid white kid under a racetrack grandstand in 1963, applause was no longer required. Now, it was one solid croon, the whole mass vocalizing together. And even with the occasional low moan, or because of it, the night foamed up. Everyone got used it. Some people moaned back. They'd hum along in pitch and pretty soon the room would vibrate with that one frequency. I wondered if all the cement would cleave apart and start raining down.

On the next break, Barney lifted the wooden gate along the bar and told us to go into the office, which was an old kitchen. There were steel vats, a scarred up oven with junk on it, a sink full of gadgets and pans, pin-up girls—all naked and splayed out in ways that I'd never imagined. Len was in there waiting, a half-eaten sandwich in front of him. He got up and asked who was in charge.

"All of us, I guess," Billy said.

"I'll give you fifty bucks if you can go to midnight."

"We'll have to repeat some songs from earlier," Billy said.

"Whatever," Len said. "Just keep it coming."

And so we did. We repeated most of the first set. No one seemed to care. If the drums kept going, Billy could yell out chords while tearing all over the neck. Eddie kept pounding and the crowd kept swirling around. The longer we went, the better it got—like we were holding everyone aloft for four minutes, five minutes, six impossible minutes. All the short songs we'd learned worked perfectly in car radios—between conversations, between commercials, between intersections. But here, the two-minute ditty wasn't nearly long enough for the exorcism that everyone needed.

By the end, people were throwing themselves around in circles, their arms out like scarecrows, their necks flopping like broken twigs. Plenty knew the popular dances—the twist, the surfer, the watusi, the hully gully, the jerk—but all that prescribed movement exploded. The designated postures fizzled away. And the fact is the music sounded like a dogfight in a garage, like a blast of electrified growling. How could anyone move according to some preconceived jitter? Even the most proper girls who'd spent quiet nights in their rooms memorizing the steps and turns let their memories go. They left their calculations and howled like she-wolves into the dank air. And the athletically poised men threw their arms out to catch the current. If anything, I can say that it worked because it was awful.

After the final boomy note, Len celebrated. He came up glistening and couldn't keep the sweat from his eyes. "This place never seen anything like it," he said—blinking after every other word. "Let's talk about the winter."

He corralled us to a table. We sat down, all of us full of a dreamy projection—no one imagining anything other than more people and more money.

"If you boys can keep doing this," Len said, "just like you did here tonight, there's reward for us all."

"That sounds good," Billy said. "What are we talking about?"

"We're talking about twice per month," Len said. "Not every week. Every other week."

"What kind of pay?" Joel asked.

"Well, there's four of you."

"How about eighty?" Billy said.

Len wasn't ready for a mathematical commitment. We could tell that much. But it didn't take a genius to figure that he'd moved a lot of beer. He hadn't seen that kind of influx from anything in years—maybe ever. We knew it. And he knew—or at least was coming to know—that we knew it. "Fuck it," he said. "Eighty bucks. But the people have to keep coming. If the numbers shrink, the pay shrinks too."

We didn't argue. We didn't care. Forty bucks a month, back then, was good—damned good for a teenager.

Billy was staring at the stage. "You know, Len, if you'd add on, we could get the whole band up there."

"The bar would have to move down," Len said.

"You could charge more," Billy said. "People way in the back could see and hear better—you know, like a real show."

Joel said he'd make the whole thing happen in a weekend. "A couple of hammers, some plywood, some nails. I'd take care of it."

"Maybe," Len said. "But I'd do better to burn the place down and start from scratch."

~

Meanwhile, Dale Krug had turned up dead—beaten and partially frozen outside a bar in Chicago. Maybe he threw a beer bottle at someone. Maybe he took a swing at the wrong dude. It doesn't matter. It was his overall plan. I'm not saying that he had it charted out: get married, blast through a dozen jobs, get green pickup, drink all the beer in the county, throw bottles everywhere, have some kids, knock them around, escape to Chicago, piss off someone bigger than me. Maniacal meanasses don't make charts. But his path to destruction was clear and direct. It's not like he was a pediatrician who happened, by a series of coincidences, to mouth off in a bar or step on someone's foot. He had to have seen it coming. And for the rest of us, the news seemed like a natural conclusion. When you hear about a guy like Dale getting beat to death outside a bar in Chicago, you're only question is, why Chicago?

Two years before, Dale had tried to run over Joel, failed at it, but then succeeded in running over a gas station. Rather than go to jail, he left his pickup and staggered away from the scene. He fled town and then the state, but his iniquities caught up with him somewhere on the east side of a dangerous city. There was no funeral. Joel's mother never went to claim the body. Even before news of Dale's death, she'd found a judge to eradicate her link to the Krug name so she could marry Ray Slagle, one of the Nazarene coots.

Joel said nothing about Dale's death. And he wanted nothing to do with his mother's new life in Edon. He wanted everything to do with Bryan—playing bass, flapping around with me, and collapsing into Helen. He didn't say, but I figured without much figuring that he and Helen had made some promises to one another. I walked into the library one afternoon and there he was, leaning back in one of those dark wooden chairs and staring at the ceiling. He had his feet up on the encyclopedias and his hands folded on his stomach.

"Hey, man," I said.

"Hey, there," he said back.

Maybe it was the posture, his comfort, the way the sun was streaming through the long window, or everything put together, but I realized that he'd been there for a while, that he and Helen were bound for something, that I was bound for something else.

~

When we didn't have instruments in our hands, and if Joel wasn't in some quiet room with Helen, we drank hard and circled the back roads of Williams County. There was something about snaking around in the darkness with town glow, like a lip, on the horizon. It made everything bigger and faraway. And on one of those nights, we ended up at Joel's shack—the place south of Edon, where he'd spent the better part of a year engulfed in kerosene fumes and field mice. I don't remember if it was circumstance or if Joel directed me to it, but there we were—my engine rumbling by a crude and listing hut.

"Fuck you," Joel said at it.

I guess the others may have been wondering, but I knew. It was that whole scabby part of his life—back when Dale's reflexes ruled.

"Let's go," Joel said.

So we took beers, got out, and headed for the porch. We stood there sipping and looking out like it was home, like we were surveying our own dark brambly domain, and that's when Joel started. He said, out of nowhere, "That's where my dad tried to run me over."

He couldn't take it back or stave off the questions. Eddie was all fisted up about it. He kept asking, so we all went twenty or thirty yards from the shack and stood knee-deep in the weeds while Joel sat down like he had years before. "I'm right here," he said, "right fucking here, minding my own business. I'm sitting in front of a perfectly nice fire, fading off—falling asleep without that kerosene stink. I hear an engine, turn around, and find myself staring into high beams. And at this point, I have no idea—no clue at all—who's aiming lights at me."

"It's your dad?" Eddie said.

"You wouldn't wanna think it," he said, "but it's the old man. It's him. I haven't seen him in days at this point, but there he is looking at me from the behind the wheel. The truck's close enough now and I see the grill and I can see his fucking face. He revs the engine. And it's not just a threat. He's not just toying with me. I know somehow. I fucking know, for some reason, to run my ass off. So I do. I start running."

And at this point, he did. He started running. We had no better option than to follow, so we were all stumbling into the dark, chasing him while he yelled out the past.

"I turn around like this, and I see the chair I was sitting in shatter. It explodes. It just blows up. Sparks go spraying out because his tires hit the fire, and I know, like I knew originally, that this is serious. I keep turning and running. The headlights pan out. I see my own shadow waving against the dark in front of me. There I am. There's me trying not to get my ass flattened. And I realize that the latrine—the goddamned crapper—is my only hope. I veer for it."

And we were all running for the old outhouse, all of us lunging like we had to go bad.

"It's the only solid object within range—and somehow, maybe because I'm supposed to make it—I make it."

And so there we were—Eddie, Lance, me, and Joel—standing by a wooden shell that was, at one point, a halfway legitimate outhouse.

"So I jump on the dark side of it, and the headlight beam comes up behind me—right up close but split in two. The engine revs. I mean, he's cranking it up to a whine, and I'm thinking, here we go. Here's the end. So I run in the opposite direction. I'm running and thinking that the headlights will smash through the crapper and come over the top of me. I'm ready to get flattened. I've got my back all tensed, my arms out like this. But when I turn around, I see the taillights—the ass-end, not the front—out by the road. The old man has given up. He's officially decided not to run me over."

"That's it? Eddie said.

"You didn't get run over?"

"Not that I recall," Joel said. "I just sat here in the weeds and listened to myself breathing. I squatted here for a good long time. It was just me and the mosquitoes enjoying me being alive."

And what Joel didn't say was that meanwhile, Dale was manhandling the steering wheel long enough make Montpelier and then the gas station, and then Chicago, and then, eventually, the alley where he finally met God.

Eddie or Lance asked straight up if Joel knew what made Dale go berserk, and Joel shrugged his shoulders. He didn't know any more than anyone, and I suspect none of us could begin to sniff out the urges in a man like Dale Krug. So we let it be and decided that the goddamned outhouse had saved Joel's life. We saluted it, announced some yea verilies, and then jubilated ourselves with more beers.

~

Over the holidays, the thing between Helen and Joel had become crackly and vibrant. You could feel it. They'd walk into rooms laughing about some secret discovery. If Eva and Nicholas were a conclave of memory, Joel and Helen were a ball of presence. They shimmered. Of course, Helen's family was devastated. They'd met Joel. They knew that he wasn't Catholic, and they knew his last name. He may as well have been a disease. Polio. Krug. Lupus. But Helen had made up her mind. There was something about Joel that kept the rest of the world at bay. One of my earliest memories—one of the first times I felt like myself—involved Joel. We were young, maybe nine or ten, and sitting in that one-room school. Bobby Kowalksi had been taped to his chair after several hours of fidgeting. Mrs. Randall made a performance of it—holding the heavy gray tape in the air, pulling out the first couple of feet so that the thwipping sound filled the room, then circling under Bobby's desk and up over his legs until his bottom half was wrapped tight like spider prey. No one was sure if Bobby could move or not, if the tape was really that strong, but he trumped Mrs. Randall when he peed the seat. While she continued with her lesson on polite language and posture, Bobby's pee ran down his leg and went cruising backward on the slope of the hardwood floor. It found a subtle dip in the boards, formed a creek, and flowed merrily along between Joel and me. As we studied its progress toward the back of the room, our heads moved slowly to the side. Over Bobby's creek, we looked into one another's eyes and shared a moment of secret knowing that ruptured only when Edie Brown saw the creek coming at her in the back row and trumpeted out "PEE!!" From that moment on, Joel and I had something. In those few seconds, we sensed the bigness of someone's urine rolling down the center of a classroom. We didn't laugh or gasp or anything. We watched and waited to see how the rest of the world would deal with it. That's what Joel did to people—not just me, not just Helen. He'd learned to create a bubble for himself and anyone who wanted in.

~

As the winter rolled, Len Polk realized the economics of rock-n-roll. He shook our hands whenever we came in. Anything we wanted, he got for us. "Fuck it, I love it." That was his admission. He said it all the time, and I wondered, fuck what? Maybe anything that got in the way. Maybe everything.

We played there every other week into March. It caught on. People from all those angry little towns—West Unity, Alvordton, Archbold, Stryker, Lyons, Hillsdale—came in packs. The older people drank like they were after something. Their eyes would get narrow. They'd squint like they were scoping a target in the distance. And there were goons. That's what we called them—the bigger, hairier, more thunderous men, not bikers because they hadn't been invented yet, not quite hillbillies or rednecks, but something else entirely. Anyone walking in on those nights would have distinguished the groups: older flatlanders looking for a shock to the system, prehistoric gangly giants looking for a reason to go blind drunk, and young howlers like us trying to leave themselves behind forever. Sure, there was some tension, but the occasional scuffle ended quickly. Someone would go down and that'd be it. People didn't pull weapons, generally speaking, and they didn't kick you when you were down. Things were different back then. Down was down. Plus, there was the music. It sucked up the wrath. In my name they shall cast out devils. They shall speak with new tongues.

Over the months, we'd brewed up a solid night—a range of shiny new songs and a few underground doozeys. The goons especially liked "Hot Nuts." When the key line came, the whole mass chanted together: "Nuts! Hot Nuts! Buy 'em from the peanut man." The beers got hoisted in a universal goon salute and the place juiced up another notch. After that, we could play anything. As long as there was an electric sizzle coming out of the amp and a pulsating sound from Eddy, the crowd kept drinking and forgetting, drinking and forgetting.

In the midst of it, Joel had become comfortable. He no longer watched Billy for the changes. He stood beside Eddie's drums, eyes closed, concentrating on that other dimension where bass players go. It's "behind the beat" Billy used to say. Joel was coming to understand it. Even back then, at that age, he was finding the crevasse behind each downbeat and just before the hint of the next. Good bass players find it, and when they do, they make the measures bigger. They're ushers. They open the door and corral the rest of us inside. It's hard work—way more than a finger game—and Joel was just beginning to make it happen. At seventeen, and only months after picking up the instrument, he was digging into layers that plenty of older guys can barely sense. I've performed with a million bass players over the years. Some of them don't have a feel for what's beneath them. They play all the right notes. They have the right sound, the right look, but they ram through each measure and never look down into the silence. Not Joel. He lived with each note like it was home.

The racetrack had become our place—where we rehearsed, stretched into new songs, drank, smoked, and imagined what was coming. In those late hours, in the fumes and cigarette smoke, we'd sit at the bar and rehash the night or mill around outside and watch the carnival of goons. One night, it was just Joel and me, the two of us with beers and cigarettes. A couple goons were hauling out their buddy—who'd maxed out. They drug him through the parking lot, his feet raking the gravel. After a little conference, which we couldn't hear, they started lifting the drunken goon onto the car like he was a piece of luggage. They got him up there, belly-down, face draping onto the windshield, and then opened the trunk.

"What in the fuck?" Joel asked me.

"Looking for rope," I figured.

"Good guess."

Apparently, there was no rope. The two goons climbed in, rolled down their windows, and grabbed an arm of the luggage goon. They did a test lurch and the car popped forward a few feet. They realized the inevitable, but rather than abandon the mission, the passenger goon propped himself up and sat on the door to get a better grip on the luggage goon.

"Much better," Joel said.

The movement of the car stirred up the luggage goon's stomach and he let loose on the windshield. After some deliberation, the driver opted for wipers but not fluid. And with a glistening cakey windshield, the car rocked its way onto the road.

"What in the hell are we doing?" Joel asked.

I knew what he meant. "Providing music," I told him. "That's all."

"Yea verily," he said.

~

At some point that winter, I don't know when, Joel asked Len if he could stay in the little room behind the stage. It was a supply closet that we'd been using for our things—equipment, tools, and extra clothes. Len had brought an old army cot in so we could change in there, relax, and get a break from the goons. Joel had developed a feel for it. Plus, the racetrack was between Bryan and the Sholwalters', who needed him despite the fact that he'd broken the deal, that he'd left school and turned heathen. And Len had no problem with Joel camping at the track. In fact, he seemed flattered. We were a jolt to Len's life. All the money, sound, energy, and women would have been fiction unless we'd brought it all with us. His place was dying—had been for years—until we came along. At one point, it'd been a restaurant with tables, a menu, waitresses, the whole deal. But he'd managed to stink up the situation and people stopped going. We gave him another chance—a final glimpse of upright humans and a swipe at their wallets. At the end of each night, he was never anxious to clear us out. He'd stand in the midst of it—one leg on the last stool of the bar, one finger stirring his drink. He'd listen, smirk a little, and lean back into the reward. Plus, he'd taken a public liking to Eva. When she and Nicholas stayed into the wee hours, he'd buy a round or two and leer—in front of a whole table, in front of Nicholas. One night, while I was at the bar next to Len's stool, he started rambling. He stared at Eva, who sat twenty feet away. I was a bystander—an intermediary. "Men are beasts," he said. "We're ugly as hell. All we want is a little beauty, to rub up against it." Then he rattled his drink at Barney.

No doubt, Eva was pretty. She was straight and precise. And she'd been through the most hell men can dream up for others. I don't think Len knew about the concentration camp, but he must have sensed something dense and faraway in her. He'd leave himself and run after it whenever she was in the room.

~

I didn't know Helen was pregnant until it was obvious. And once it was obvious, everyone turned inside-out. Whatever fears or hopes were swimming under the skin came busting through the surface. I know little about the debates at the Peterson farm. I can picture Helen's father leaning against the kitchen threshold shaking his freckled head at the floor, her mother wringing her hands around a coffee cup, and of course the networks of quiet talk—the rivulets of gossip from Nazarenes, Catholics, Blakesleens, and Montpelierites all merging into one condemnation.

Those days were maddening for Joel. He was flush and fidgety, waiting to hear from Helen, waiting to know how to act or react. He smoked a lot, drove around, marched up and down High Street. I tried to tow him in. I asked him to stay at Billy's. I offered my room. Billy said he could have the run of the place. Lance said the same. But Joel heard nothing. His brain was full of white noise. He wanted to be out there on the rim of town, closer to Helen who'd moved back to the farm. He didn't want comfort or sleep. He wanted to be alert, ready for something. One night, we met up and he had bloody knuckles. I asked what happened.

"Some asshole with a big mouth," he said.

"You okay?" I asked.

And he answered by telling me that he understood the Petersons' concerns. "I'm Krug," he said.

I asked him what he meant. I knew but asked anyway.

"Think of Eric Watson's mom."

"She was an asshole," I said. "And she's probably dead."

"Yea verily."

"Double yea verily," I said.

"But still. I'm Krug."

Joel carried that around with him. His mother married it away. His older brother moved into the rolling anthills of southern Michigan where the Krug name was a sound like any other. But Joel lived with it. He was the last of the Krugs.

We all had suggestions and offers. Billy said Helen and Joel could move in with him. Lance said the same thing—that he'd clear the whole second floor so they'd have plenty of room. The kid, he said, would grow up with music and bonfires. He almost begged. Nicholas and Eva said they'd be godparents. And we all dreamed that it would be okay—despite the fact that we knew nothing at all. We were ready to help. But in the middle of the morning, in the middle of a week in April, the fire trucks made a fortress around the racetrack grandstand. By sunrise, the firemen retreated from the charred cement steps. Joel's car was in the parking lot but he was never found.

Helen had an aunt in California, and that's where she went. It's not hard to imagine the reasons. I got an address and wrote long letters. Nothing came back. I couldn't picture her on the West coast—mountains blooming up around her, constant sun, an ocean in the distance. I don't blame her for leaving, for being quiet, or for losing track. Some people stay on the ground and get plowed into it. They mix with the soil and the roots. Others fly away. They go shooting out away from time, from what happened and will happen. Helen was a flyer. I was. Joel was too.

That summer, we wandered around numb and stupefied. We tried to sit down together and kick up some energy, but everything felt done. One night, Eddie tried to rile us into a posse—mustering up our baddest juices, barging into Len's trailer, and forcing a confession. Nicholas and Eva supported it. In fact, Eva was hellbent. She said it was the right thing to do. She paced in Lance's kitchen and described the process—how we'd take two cars, gag Len, stick him in a trunk, and drive him to the woods. She said she'd get to the truth in minutes. But Lance shut it down. He said we were delusional, that grief was making us crazy. He was right, and we proved it to ourselves.

On a wet night in June, Eddie and I drove out to see Nicholas and Eva. We were hanging around in their little cabin at the back end of that chicken farm. They didn't have enough chairs for us all, so Eddie and I sat on the wood floor, let our beers sweat next to us, and listened to Eva and Nicholas theorize about their poultry business—how they were saving up for a place, how they'd build a better coop, raise better chickens, really make a go of it.

Someone brought up Len—how he was living out there with a barrel of insurance money, grand plans to rebuild, and so on, and that stoked Eva. She stood up and looked at us flat-faced. "Let's go," she said.

We all looked at her.

"Well?" she said.

Eddie stood up next. He looked at me, and I knew that it was all going to happen. Maybe, as they say, it was the heat. Maybe we all just needed fresh air.

We left the cabin and piled in my car. I remember going around Bryan, not through, thinking that the longer drive would conjure some options, something other than the obvious. It didn't work. In fact, the dark drive north of town—plenty far from streetlights and infrastructure—woke up the monsters in us.

Len's trailer sat a few hundred yards from the burnt up grandstand. It was all alone out there, one hovel in a big field. I shut off the headlights as we came down the road and parked in the gravel lot where we'd always hung around before the show. I killed the engine and we sat in silence. We didn't have a plan, just balled-up rage. We took it and walked across the field, through wet thistles and over old bottles. I had a few second thoughts, and maybe everyone else did too, but the car was getting further away, and there was nothing else to do with ourselves, nowhere else to be. So standing there a few feet from Len's door, in the dull glow of a livingroom lamp, we started whispering a plan together. Eddie wanted to drag him out in the open, which didn't make any sense to me. Eva was focused on some kind of kidnapping, and Nicholas settled it all by telling us—in a full-throated whisper—that we were going in to talk. "We'll just talk," he said. And that felt reasonable.

Odd as it seems, Len came to the door when we knocked. He looked through the screen and told us to come in. It was late, and we weren't exactly invited guests, but he told us to take a seat at the table, which was perfectly clean. In fact, the whole place was tidy as hell. It smelled like potpourri—cinnamon and rose petals—and there was a full bookshelf that went to the ceiling. You can't imagine how people live.

Nicholas, Eddie, and I took seats at the table. Len went to his recliner—a big blue puffy thing where he'd probably spent most of his life—and Eva stood in the place between.

"We want to know about the fire," she said.

Len nodded. He wasn't surprised or put off. He moved his head up and then down, once each.

"How did it start?" Eddie said from the table.

"I wouldn't know," Len said.

And before anyone could take a breath, Eva was standing over him. "You do know," she said. "And you're going to tell us."

He looked up at her—placid, comfortable, and maybe glad that her body was nestled in so close, her breasts hanging inches from his mouth. He said nothing.

"What happened to Joel?" Eddie said.

"I wouldn't know that either," Len said—still looking up at Eva, taking in every second of her proximity, reveling in it.

I don't remember who said what, but something made Eva press Len's head back into his chair. Nicholas, Eddie, and I watched from the table. She put the heel of her palm against his forehead and pushed hard. And once the chair slammed back against the wall, we all got up. We gathered around him and watched his face clench. Eva kept applying pressure. She leaned into it like she was trying to move the whole trailer with Len's head.

"What happened to Joel," Eddie said. "What happened?"

But Len's head was getting crushed and his jaws were clenched. After a few minutes like that—his forehead squeezing down into this eyes, his glasses pinching his nose shut—he started seething and spitting through his teeth, and that's when Nicholas intervened. He pulled Eva back. She'd turned into a bulldozer, but he managed to cradle her arms from behind, to slowly shut down her engines until Len's chair flopped forward and back into place.

There were a couple minutes of hard breathing—Len looking straight ahead, his glasses still down, his shirt coming up over his chin. I wondered what would happen next, how we'd end it. Most of me figured Len was halfway dead already, that his heart was exploding, that the rest of him was waiting for the concussion.

"Here's the thing," Nicholas said. "We weren't here."

Len kept staring ahead.

"Hey!" Nicholas said. "Look at me."

Len moved his eyes up.

"We were never here. And if you say anything different—anything about this—we'll be back. We'll be back, okay?"

Len didn't say okay or anything, but he bobbed his head the smallest bit. He understood. For Eva, it wasn't over. She kept saying that we knew, that we'd be watching. And with her saying so, we let ourselves out, walked across the field, got in my car, and drove away.

After that, I worried about Nicholas and Eva. They were easy targets—Russians, farm laborers, people who talked funny. I told them both to lay low, and then I told Nicolas separately because it seemed like Eva wasn't hearing me. "Don't let her," I told him. "Keep her away from there."

"I don't know that I can stop her," he said.

"Then tie her to a post," I said.

He laughed a little, but I was serious. "At least for a while," I told him. And it must have worked. I know it did.

In late August, the 28th to be exact, around 11:00, Len got himself killed. It was a small headline, barely a whimper. The paper suggested some kind of bail bond scheme, which was conjecture. It also said he was shot in his home, and that part was true. "Cause of death, a shotgun wound to the abdomen." That was also true. And as far as I know, no arrests were made or attempted. Yea verily.

That fall, Sarah and Lance got married. Nicholas and Eva got a small place, a farm with one coop, just over the border in Michigan. Billy realized that he was geared for men and said so. Word of that traveled like a radio wave. His family barked and pecked at him until he launched himself out of the area and landed somewhere on the East coast. I never found out where, but I was glad to see him escape. Eddie moved up to Detroit. I was hoping he'd go further, but Detroit made some sense. As for me, I just drifted off in wider circles—Indianapolis, Nashville, Memphis, then Little Rock, Austin, Tampa, Richmond, New York, anywhere but home, anywhere but home. For a while, I tried to find Helen. I imagined meeting her child, having a chance to say something about Joel—about that frenzied year and all the carousing flatlanders who swirled around us. But I gave that up. At some point, I realized that Joel's story would find its own way, that I'd done and said enough.

I've spent my life on stage—performing, singing for throngs of people who know my voice. Year after year, decade on decade, I sold myself to anyone who'd listen. But I've kept my secrets. And I've never gone back. I won't do it, not in this skin. Occasionally, I spend time in Chicago, only a few hours from that little splotch of flatland. Once I considered driving through, but I let the idea fizzle away. In the end, we all scattered. We took our guilt and wonder and went into the world alone. Maybe that was rock-n-roll's job—to drive things to their end, to turn people and all their contraptions into smoke.

The Moles

I've always been like this. At least since I was fourteen or so, I've been waving goodbye from my own little raft. Everyone keeps shrinking. And for some reason, I can't make myself care enough to start paddling back. I can admit that my actions haven't always been humane. That's the word a judge used on me—humane. "Human with an *e* on the end," he said, as though I were some kind of monkey, as though I hadn't any familiarity with the language that spills out of my own mouth. That same judge asked me right there in the courtroom, after I'd made a mess of a motel in Alvordton, if I knew the origin of my transgressions. He thought his question was a revelation.

I said nothing in return. I stood there in cuffs and let him think what he needed to think. I let him squint the way people do, like they're trying to see past your skin and observe some core malady by force of their own virtue. Of course, I could have told him. I could explained what I know, what I've concluded about myself. I knew the answer to his question. I've known for years.

It goes back to my sister's moles. Our mother called them freckles, but they weren't freckles. They demanded more attention than that. They announced themselves from a distance. They made a bracelet on Ruth's left wrist, snaked around her neck, lined her shins, and in plain sight of everyone, they formed a constellation T on her right forearm. And based on the coverage of her visible parts, I assumed they covered her torso as well. They appeared when she was four or five, and I guess doctors today would have an explanation for that. Back then, we didn't.

In elementary school, nobody said much. Kids that age have their own problems—especially out where we lived. There were so many snaggletooths, hairlips, and bugeyes that a quiet girl with moles got mostly overlooked. But pretty soon, kids get comfortable. By their teen years, they open their eyes and realize that the world is tilted, that if you don't start climbing, you're going to spend your life on the side that's dipping down into the hurt. And that's what happened.

In middle school, a few of Ruth's classmates called her "spot" and it caught on. Before long, she was one of those kids on the bottom of the slope—a girl who marks the difference between the lucky and the cursed. They hollered all kinds of things, and I heard enough of the echoes that it made me knock some heads. One kid, Tony Mallard, deemed her the school leopard. By the time I got to him, his invention had already traveled around. I roughed him up, but I was only one set of arms. I couldn't stave off the smirks and all those things that whirl around in the breeze. I couldn't but I most definitely—and with some consequence—tried my best. I got good at pegging the loudmouths and jumping them after school. I got my point across most often, but I also got stomped a couple times—when three or four kids decided they'd combine efforts.

And so middle school years took their toll. Ruth and I were spent up—drained of the tolerance and curiosity it takes to get

along with people. I was dreading high school, but it turned out
that Ruth was dreading it more. Just before the year started, she
jumped a train—one of those slow movers headed for Chicago.
She mostly made it, but in one of those big railroad yards outside
of the city, she got nabbed by a night watchman and turned over
to the police. On the drive home, somewhere along in Indiana,
Ruth said she wasn't going back to school. She wanted to disappear into a city. "I want to be a nobody," she said, and I guess
that's how our mother decided to take action. The day after that,
she put Ruth in the car, told me to stay put, and drove out to
Gene Whitman's place.

Whitman wasn't a preacher in the formal sense. He filled in
at the Nazarene whenever the real preacher was off somewhere
on holiday or just taking a morning away from the congregation.
When Whitman filled in, things were different. He didn't con-
demn people or insist that we were doomed to lakes of fire. He
whispered at us, told us all the time that God was waiting. He said
it like a secret. He said God was always asking the question—Are
you ready yet? Are you ready now? He said that God was waiting
in between the flaps of a butterfly's wings. I remember that.

Most people, even those outside of the Nazarene, knew Whitman as a healer. He'd once brought an old woman, Marigold
Holloway was her name, from the brink. She'd been bedrid-
den for weeks. Pneumonia had taken all her strength and was
poised for victory when Whitman went to the house and turned
ordinary vinegar into a potion. The story goes that he murmured incantations while waving his hand over the vinegar and
then poured the stuff gently into her mouth. She woke from a
near-death sleep, coughed up three handkerchiefs of dark green
phlegm, and made the bed she'd almost died in. The next day,
she was in her yard raking leaves. That's my telling of course, but

it's no different than how I'd heard it countless times, so I guess that's what happened.

I also heard that Whitman watched over the Blakeslee cemetery at night and chased off demons who'd come looking for souls of the freshly dead. I can't say whether that's true or not.

So Ruth and my mother were gone for the evening. When they came back, I was asleep on the couch. I don't remember much from that night, but I remember the next morning—coming out and seeing Ruth. Her neck, legs, and wrist were one color. Pure skin. "Ruther," I asked, "what happened?"

She didn't really know. "That doctor out there cured my freckles," she said. I couldn't tell if she was happy or confused or everything all at once. I figure she'd prepared herself for one path or the other—running away or tunneling through another year of sorrow—and now she had to rethink her options.

We started school. The days rolled along and nobody said anything about the moles being gone. A few weeks in, I was standing against the lockers with Malcolm Jennings—a lanky troll of a guy who got his share of abuse. Across from us, Tony Mallard and his gaggle were standing around. Just before the bell rang, Ruth came walking down the hall. I watched Mallard elbow one of his buddies, look Ruth up and down, and then give one of those approving nods. As his head was still bobbing up and down, he caught my eye and I caught his. It took a few teachers and several of Mallard's buddies to pull me off, but not before I beat him until his nose was about gone, and that's when the school decided that I wasn't worth educating. They sent me down to a special place in Bryan where I stayed for a year and a few months. I quit the week after I turned sixteen.

Ruth died a couple years ago in a car wreck. She was up in Hillsdale, lost control on some ice, went off the road, and slammed into a tree. She was alone. Not even the tree suffered. That's what I thought back when I went up to the site and stood around trying to remember everything I could about Ruth. She didn't hurt anyone. She lived, and then she died.

I'm not saying that Ruth's moles made me what I am—that her ailment or Tony Mallard caused me to trash that motel lobby or anything else I've done. I'm not trying to duck retribution. I'm just answering the question. Do I know the origin of my transgressions? I think that I do. And if I had to tell that judge something, I'd mention Gene Whitman. People might say that what he did for Ruth was humane, that he saved her life in a way, and that's a fine thing to say—as good as any other. But when he fixed her, he made everything clear. He showed the truth and proportion of things. People are terrible. Kids are worse yet. It takes magic to make them otherwise.

The Groundlings

They concluded that Ran Manville had shimmied up the maple tree, crawled across the one low limb, and heaved himself onto Gwendolyn Lutz's roof. As to why, no one had a good answer. It didn't make much sense—a guy like him perched on a roof and singing Just Tell Her Jim Said Hello so the whole neighborhood could hear. Granted, he was a little touched, in Tommy Pahl's words, but Ran Manville didn't seem like the type to express himself in such an outward manner or shimmy his way up anything. Helen Wheeler claimed it was some kind of romantic gesture. Calvin Sumner blamed the humidity— unprecedented soupy air that had been hanging around for weeks. Muriel Wonsettler called it a ritual of some sort. Her husband dismissed that out-of-hand and argued that not everything has to be a ritual. "Some things," he said, "are just what they are." Marigold Holloway blamed it on liquor and no one disagreed. After all, Jacob McComby's latest batch of superhooch had been making its way around.

But the real question was how to get Ran Manville down. No one had shared more than a few words with him in recent years.

He lived out there near the St. Joe and mostly kept to himself. He'd been a calm boy and then a handsome teenager. But in his twenties, something happened. His face expanded. He took on cumulus dimensions. His razor jaw disappeared, his marble eyes receded into a field of cakey flesh, and the thin-lipped smirk that had given him an aura of vitality in his teen years turned into a dunderheaded smile that made people reach quick conclusions. "Not a quite a retard" is how Calvin Sumner put it.

Sheriff VanGundy pulled up around 11:00. They watched him sit in the patrol car, study the roof, put on his hat, and get out. He nodded in their direction and walked up to the front porch where Gwendolyn Lutz met him. They couldn't hear the back and forth, but the conversation didn't seem like a good one—plenty of head shaking and staring at the porch floor.

The sheriff went around back, and Muriel Wonsettler brought up the fact that there'd been an accident out on 576 already that morning—that a couple of kids were racing and drove each other into a ditch, which was probably why the sheriff was so late on the scene and pretty haggard. And then Murray Wonsettler brought up the Ronnie LeCroix situation from the spring before. Everyone knew the story—how Ronnie got himself drunk, went out to the Gregorys' pond, and announced that he was repossessing it on behalf of his ancestors. The sheriff had to intervene not only to keep Mr. Gregory from using his shotgun but also to pull Ronnie LeCroix from the water after he'd jumped in and sank. Granted, there was currently a 250-pound man perched on a roof, singing, and probably—almost certainly—drunk. But the sheriff had seen worse. Everyone agreed on that point.

Even though they couldn't see Ran from the grass, they knew he was way at the top—not on the mudroom but the main slope a good forty feet up. Gwendolyn Lutz's house was one of those brick two-stories with a full attic, made at the turn of the century—back when people built toward the sky.

"Especially out here on the flatland," Murray Wonsettler said.

"Especially out here," Calvin Sumner said. "Anything to get away from the ground."

And Muriel added they wouldn't be able to strong-arm Ran if it came to that. The slope was too much. Someone would fall.

"It's likely."

"Definitely likely."

By noon, the sheriff had conscripted the Wonsettlers' ladder and climbed onto the mudroom. He stood with his face at the lip of the main roof trying to communicate with Ran, but it was a one-way channel. From the grass, everyone could see the top of Ran's head and how he was scuttling away—casually scooting off like those pileated woodpeckers that know, somehow, exactly where your vision ends. That's how Tommy Pahl described it. And everyone nodded or kept thoughts to themselves because they could hear movement—Ran's shoes or pants scraping the shingles as he made progress along the peak. And then he appeared, his whole girth finally and fully visible, now resting against the chimney. He held the jug of hooch, sure enough, and stared out over the houses.

The sun crested the two giant cottonwoods on the east side of the street and shone on Ran's body curled up against the bricks. Marigold brought up heat stroke. "Someone," she said, "had better get up there and pull him down." Frank Mallard agreed. "They wait too much longer and they may as well get a gurney." Calvin Sumner wondered why they wouldn't get the fire department—the cherry picker or even one of those trampolines. Tommy Pahl said they should let Ran fall asleep, which was bound to happen, and then roll off because quite often people don't get injured if they're entirely limp. The impact, he said, goes right through the skeletal system and into the air. Helen Wheeler thought they should bring out a couple of semi-truck trailers and park them on either side of the house. Muriel Wonsettler said they'd never get Mrs. Lutz to allow such destruction to her lawn and ceramics. And Frank Mallard said someone with authority had to end this foolery even if it meant getting out the handcuffs and billystick. "You have to take control," he said. "That's a sheriff's job."

And so the talk turned to Sheriff VanGundy and his particular reflexes. There was the problem a few months back at Shorty's Grill involving the group from Indiana who felt like they could push some locals around and then come back the following week and do the same. And there was the situation with Greta Stenson two years prior. She'd announced plans to kill her husband—explaining her intentions to everyone within earshot. And rather than intervene, Sheriff VanGundy let it happen. "I can't stop a woman from telling stories," he said. So like Greta promised, she pierced Michael Stenson through the abdomen when he tried to mount her without asking. The weapon—as most people had heard—was Michael Stenson's own scaling knife.

By late afternoon, nearly everyone in town who wasn't working had gathered on Avondale Drive to listen for Ran Manville's voice—how it would blather out another line or two from that same song, the one he'd been singing in arrhythmic starts and stops for at least six hours. It had become sloppier, like he was arguing. In the lapses people nodded their heads, agreeing that he'd finally succumbed to the liquor and heat. But then a warbling tone would start up and roll out over the lawns. Marcus Jennings explained that Ran had surpassed normal human tolerance for heat. The Wonsettlers, who had a daughter in medicine, agreed. Ran Manville was plenty beyond what a body could take. There was some kind of endurance stored up inside him.

Not everyone remembered seeing Ran grow into the thick and loafy creature above them. But Marigold Holloway said what a few others were thinking. Little Randolph Manville was one of those kids from the Church of the Nazarene, the one that Lorna Ferrick cursed with a bucket of river mud. It had been twenty years. Plenty of people never knew about the curse in the first place, and plenty had let it flutter away. There wasn't any proof. No one could say for sure that Lorna Ferrick did what some said. But it was hard not to see a pattern—how the Polk kids flamed out early, how the Housmans withered away, and how the other Manvilles went crazy or off to jail. And it wasn't hard to look at Randolph, the youngest in the family, and imagine that something unnatural had happened. There was a deep kind of trouble in all that flesh.

As the sun carved its way toward the fields, Gwendolyn Lutz joined the huddle, which had moved further into the grass where the Wonsettlers' house created a valley of shade. There was lemonade. Frank Mallard brought a flask and sweetened things up for anyone who wasn't offended. And Mrs. Lutz explained that the sheriff had finally made a decision—that he could no longer hope for a natural resolution. Marigold said it was about time. Calvin Sumner agreed. He said that getting hurt was a risk you take for coming around and terrorizing a single woman, a widow for that matter. "That's the risk of birddoggin," he said.

Muriel Wonsettler asked Mrs. Lutz if she intended on pressing charges. Marigold Holloway answered for her, saying she'd better get something on the books or else Ran's excursion to her roof might well turn into something else, like, according to Marcus Jennings, an excursion into the livingroom. No one asked Mrs. Lutz why Ran had climbed up there—if she knew why, if she had a guess, if she wanted to offer one. No one asked but everyone watched the back of her head while she studied her own house. And Frank Mallard took the opportunity to get an eyeful—standing, as he was, behind and a little to the east where he could see the silhouette of hamstring—until he caught Marigold Holloway's eyes watching his.

Calvin Sumner decided he'd had enough standing, said so, and then walked off to join the sheriff. Twenty minutes later, they both came walking up the ally dragging a bare mattress, which flopped, resisted, and tried to pour itself free as they shoved it upward and onto the mudroom roof. From the ground, everyone understood the plan. They'd drag Ran to the mudroom. If he got too squirmy, they'd muscle him on down, let him flop the five or six feet and land, at the least, on some cushion. "It's not like that ape's made of glass," Frank Mallard said.

They waited. They felt an end coming, and it came in the form of Calvin Sumner's body. They watched it spiral over the peak, tumble toward them, drop, and thunk onto Gwendolyn Lutz's lawn. Other than Muriel Wonsettler's outstretched right hand, an attempt, maybe, to grip the scene and twist it into something else, everyone stood like pillars. They watched the sheriff jump onto the mattress. They heard him yelling while he crashed his way down the ladder and ran to the Calvin Sumner's side. They stood back because the sheriff's hand was giving them the stop signal—shoving at them through the air. They didn't turn away or move forward. They watched Calvin Sumner's body stay bent and crumpled until the ambulance arrived, until two men in gray uniforms wedged a wooden plank into the grass and lifted him away. They watched the ambulance pull off, its sirens piercing the calm humidity. Marigold Holloway whispered something about the Sumner children—both so young. And before anyone could figure something else to say, they looked to see Sheriff VanGundy already up the ladder, lifting himself onto the main roof, disappearing behind the peak. They heard three gunshots— a shot and then silence, another shot, more silence, and then a final shot.

The Tide

Marigold Holloway listened closely whenever God spoke to her among the apple trees. After coffee, she'd trace the perimeter of the back field and come up through a narrow row that curtained off the Johnson farm to the south and a clump of woods to the north. On most days, it was just Marigold, the knobby trees, and the birds. But sometimes, she'd hear the singular reedy note. At first, it was a drone—a nasal vibration like the sound of a bassoon. Then it would open into calm and ordered words.

Over the years, the voice had told Marigold about her husband's cancer and how it would outsmart the doctors, the pneumonia that would take her aunt in the middle of a snowstorm, and then the birthday cake for Dana Mueller that would turn into a kitchen fire, a house fire, then a problem for the whole block. And in the spring of '58, when the lilacs were blooming all at once, Marigold heard the bassoon again. A nighttime rain had come and gone. The ground was still wet. Marigold was standing in the corridor when she heard the drone and then the words, "They will bring their venom." She waited for more. There was nothing, not even the screech of blue jays.

"They will bring their venom," she said back.

Two days later, she stood by the potato bin in Risers Grocery. It was like any weekday—quiet and methodical. Myrna Richardson was in Natalie Tolaski's checkout lane, talking about every affliction in her vast body—a stinging all the way down her right leg, awful stomach cramps the night before, and sore feet getting sorer every day. Myrna wondered if Risers might consider a delivery service. Natalie said she didn't know, but what she did know was that next week, for the first time ever, they were going to sell bottled beer.

"Well, how about that?" Myrna said.

"They've been working at it for a year," Natalie said. "Finally got approval."

"What took so long?"

"Wheelin and dealin."

"I hope it goes good." That's what Myrna said before grabbing the handles of her canvas sack and teetering toward the door.

Marigold looked down at the potato in her hand. It had too many eyes. She put it in the bin and pressed until she felt her thumb rupture the skin. At the register, she unloaded her basket. "So you'll be selling liquor?" she said.

"Just bottles of beer. As early as next week is what Lewis says."

"After all these years," Marigold said.

So there it was. They'd sell liquor along with flour, eggs, packaged meat, and everything else. They'd stock it in the refrigerator, and all the men would come in from the fields before closing time, lumber to the back, push aside the eggs, and reach for their venom.

Other than an occasional broken bag of flour and the way Natalie Tolaski fidgeted with her own fingers while ringing up your items, Risers had been a good store. They were good people—

Mary and Lewis. They'd bought the place from that old stray dog Merrill Jacobs and turned it into a reputable business. For going on twenty years, through bad weather or tragedy, Marigold had been coming in every week, sometimes twice. And now this. She wouldn't support it, even if it meant going without. Liquor had killed Daniel after all. She'd warned him over and over, told him it was death in a bottle. He wouldn't listen. She told him, at the least, he had to keep it out of the house. Sometimes, when he was in the shed, she'd pass the bottles on the porch, reach down and feel the temperature. When you go heating up yeast, it gets a mind of its own. That's what she told him, but he laughed out loud right there on a sun-colored afternoon no less than a month before his doctor first noticed something awry.

On the way home, Marigold's decision tightened up. She figured she'd restart milk delivery with Benner's and get eggs from the Holbrook farm. Risers could go on without her. Of course, her neighbors wouldn't care much—the Richardsons, Polks, and the rest. They were glad to roll along in the wind. Like fallen leaves, they'd pile themselves into whatever nook would hold them. When the highway people raised the speed limit on Route 34, everyone grumbled and said there'd be accidents. Sure enough, there were collisions and skid-outs and funerals. When the Johnsons brought in those trailers and parked them by the road, people said it'd make the town look rotten. Years later, it looked nothing but that. And when the river flooded, everyone twiddled their thumbs. No one proposed channeling the overflow away from town. At least the state officials could have tried, but they didn't, and no one made them. The most people in Blakeslee would do about anything was shake their heads—as if Peter himself was looking down and keeping track of yeas and nays. But not Marigold Holloway. She wouldn't stand for liquor up next to the eggs. She'd go to Bryan, to that Miller market on the edge of town. It had been a while, going on five years, since she'd made the drive, but it wasn't far, only a few miles to the big curve and then a few more beyond that. She had a dependable car, a Plymouth that Daniel had kept clean, oiled, running quietly for years.

The next Monday, honeysuckle hung in the air long past sunrise. Marigold left at 10:00, enough time to get back before the men in pickup trucks would roll into town looking for lunch. She inhaled the wet grass and fresh fertilizer sneaking through the vents. She looked out at the yellow-green sprouts blanketing the fields and felt good about the day—getting out of the mile-long stretch where she'd nestled for so long, going on four years now. There were times when she and Daniel would cross into Indiana and snake around the inland lakes, back when a car ride felt like a windy dream. And today felt a little like then. The ditch weeds blurred past and the fields sprawled into the distance. Marigold pressed her toe against the pedal. Hardly anyone passed because she motored right along—over 45 on the straightaways and plenty fast on the curves.

At the big store in Bryan, the carts were shiny and clean, the aisles plenty wide. There were whole stretches of boxed cereal, shelves stacked with different colors and brands—Sugar Jets, Trix, Frosted Os—all with laughing figures and toys inside. Even the canned goods aisle was packed with options—tomato soup alone spanning out for several paces. And there were so many flashy gimmicks, so many distractions, but Marigold Holloway wasn't the type to be cajoled. She had her favorites and they were plenty visible. In front of the applesauce, a stock boy asked if she needed help. She said she didn't, but being asked—especially out of the blue—made her take extra time. She re-read labels that she knew well enough and even bought a can of beets from Minnesota. The whole affair took more time but the floor shimmered with gentle currents that caressed her ankles and the metal handle felt cool as faucet water.

The cashier was a young redhead—the flitty hot-to-trot type, the kind who was proud of her own curves, who'd likely end up in trouble. She had little to say, not because she was concentrating but because she was romancing the bagger. She'd take an item, ring it up, and push it along the metal slope so that her fingers kept touching his. With each can or box, they made sure to brush skin—even after Marigold caught the bagger's eye. And the redhead was so caught up in the touchy feelies that she pushed $1.49 instead of $.49 for the package of ground beef. When Marigold pointed it out, the girl said she didn't think so. Marigold watched the rest of the groceries get bagged and then checked the receipt. Sure enough, she pointed out the error in black and white, and being more wind than muster like most redheads, the girl didn't know how to undo what she'd done. While the manager came over and pushed the right buttons, Marigold looked back at the three women in line, all of them craning their necks and squinting.

On the way home, she came up behind a tractor. She stayed close and watched the farmer bob in mechanical rhythm, his shirt fluttering like a denim flag. She watched bullets of dried clay arc out from the tires and thought of those times when she and her sisters would chase monarchs through milkweed—and that one afternoon in particular when she, Ellen, Melissa, and the lanky Manville boy from down the road locked arms like a plow and kicked up a wave of grasshoppers in front of them. That was all before Ellen ran away, before Melissa fell from the barn roof and never got up, and before all these telephone wires.

The farmer started windmilling his left arm but Marigold couldn't see around him. He slowed down and got over, almost to the ditch. Still, there wasn't enough room. When the farmer shrugged his shoulders and threw his hands in the air, that didn't bother Marigold. "Okay," she said. "Fine with me too."

~

Two weeks later, the heavy heat of summer had arrived. By 10:00, the air inside the Plymouth had turned to syrup. Marigold stood with the door open and let the fresh air eddy through the interior. She wouldn't drive with the windows down because she didn't like the scraping noise, how it would bully her out of a quiet mood, so on the way to Bryan, she kept the passenger window halfway down and the driver side up. When she pulled into the lot, she was glistening and, truth be told, a little sticky.

She needed a range of canned goods—green beans, butter beans, peas, applesauce, peaches in syrup, and some pears. And this week, she was going to make up a little spaghetti pasta. Sure, it was hot, and pasta could be heavy in the stomach, but she always liked spaghetti in the summer—how the oregano wafted through the house, how it mixed with wet grass and livestock feed that blew in from the west. And some cottage cheese, she decided. Just a couple bites in the late afternoon would settle any discomfort brought on by the acids of sleepless nights.

In the dairy section, she stared at the milk—all different kinds, even jugs of chocolate mixed up and ready to drink. And there was a whole compartment of brick cheese—Swiss, cheddar, Colby, more choices than people needed. She looked down the aisle for a worker. There was no one in an apron, and the next three aisles were empty too. She left her cart and went to the

checkout lanes where all four cashiers were punching in numbers. There was a boxed-in raised office by the entrance but she
couldn't get to it without going through the lanes. She stood for
a good minute until she realized how she looked—a confused
old gal from Blakeslee out of tune with the bustling affairs of a
big-town store.

She picked the oldest cashier, a thin brunette in lane three,
squeezed past a woman in line, said "pardon me" because she
didn't want to be rude, and asked in a simple phrase, "Cottage
cheese?"

The cashier kept punching numbers.

She asked again, this time with more air behind it. "Cottage
cheese?"

The cashier looked up. The woman had a nice hairdo but an
empty dunderheaded gaze—just like Daniel's sister. You'd ask
her a question and have to wait a few seconds for the words to
collect themselves up in her brain.

"Dairy aisle!" the woman said.

Marigold went back to her cart. Cottage cheese could wait
until next time.

~

On Sunday, Pastor Michael was gone. Some family business
had kept him down in Chillicothe, so the service was led by
Gene Whitman, a craning boney Dutchman who'd been living
north of town—just before the Michigan border—for as long as
anyone could remember. Whitman made people uneasy because
he sometimes said things that weren't in the Bible, and when
he did, the left corner of his mouth went up. The smirk was the
sign. Even if you didn't know the Good Book, you could tell by

the smirk when Gene Whitman was going off the rails. Still, Marigold didn't mind. Whitman had a knowledge of God, plain and simple. If you couldn't see it, that was your own problem.

Whitman ended with a breathless sermon. He said that God was up close and waiting for an answer, that the question was always and forever the same. "Are you ready?" He kept asking it aloud. "And because we live this earthly life," he said, "we have to keep answering. God is waiting. He is there in between the inhale and exhale, behind each rain drop, at the bottom of the treacherous canyon and between each slip that drags us down, between a butterfly's heartbeats, between this word and its silence. He is waiting to scoop us up and away." And he asked again, "Are you ready?"

Marigold kept saying yes in her mind and then in her mouth. She felt the question quilting her shoulders, folding up around her head, and she told God that she'd always been ready. She said in whispers that she'd wait, that she'd keep listening out among the apple trees, that she'd do His will, whatever it may be. And when she opened her eyes, Whitman was sitting next to her.

"How are you, Marigold?"

"I feel good, Pastor. I feel good today."

"You're getting on okay at home?"

"Oh, sure. I get on just fine."

"Despite the hardships, I suppose we're all doing fine," he said.

"That's right. That's exactly right."

"Time was," he said looking around the empty pews, "when people would stay after service and talk a while."

"Well, people don't worship like they used to."

"I suppose not. But they worship in their own way."

"I don't know what way that would be, Pastor. I really don't. That's not a very Christian thing to say, but I said it."

"I'll grant you," he said, "these are hard times for the reverent."

"Well, that's the truth," Marigold said. She looked straight ahead and kept her hands folded over her pocketbook. "And now," she told him, "they're selling that venom at the grocery store.

"Venom?"

"Liquor. Right along with everything else."

"I didn't know. At Risers?"

There was a patient silence. Marigold imagined Whitman brooding on it, probing all the dimensions and consequences. She imagined him castigating himself for not knowing, for shopping there recently. And she imagined him seeing the future, a dark time when men would wander the streets with half-open eyes, when the righteous would be driven to far corners in search of peace.

"Well," Whitman said into the quiet, "you can't stop the tide."

Marigold stared up at the cross. The sun streams slanted in through the east windows. "Why not?" she asked. "Why can't you?"

"Because it's the tide, Marigold. It rolls around your feet and on up to the shore."

The next day, Marigold was out of orange juice. She could have gone to Risers, just a quick in and out, but she shooed the idea away. At 10:30, she was headed for Bryan, and this time, she was going to get that cottage cheese. She wouldn't ask any cashiers. She'd walk along the dairy aisle and look for herself. And that's what she did. She started at the back and scanned each compartment. First came the milk, then two full doors of cheese, and then the eggs.

"Looking for something specific, ma'am?" a stock boy said.

"Well, yes. Where's your cottage cheese?"

"That's all the way to the front."

"I guess I hadn't made it that far."

"It can be a little confusing, I suppose," he said walking along beside her.

"I think I'd put it right back there with the other cheese," she said.

"I agree with you," he said a little quieter.

Now, here was a nice young man. He had a nice haircut, none of those bangs or slick sides, and none of that swagger.

"Okay," he said. "Right here."

Marigold looked to see her favorite Daisy brand neighboring up to a compartment of beer, all those colorful bottles of Old Crown with the highfalutin lettering and shiny gold labels. Down the aisle, a woman in a snazzy skirt perused the sour cream. The registers at the front kept dinging against the music, a chirpy violin melody, and for the first time in years, Marigold's arms ached the way they did after Daniel died, that same dull and ruminant throb, something she came to understand after so many quiet mornings—not arthritis, not sore muscles, but her old bones grieving, yearning for what's gone.

"Is there one I can get for you?" he said.

"No, thank you," Marigold said turning her cart.

"It's right here, ma'am. Three different kinds."

"I changed my mind."

On 34, she heard the gurgle of racing engines. In her mirror, she saw two cars undulating on the dips of highway behind her. The first passed like a blaze. When the second started cutting back into her lane, Marigold clung to the wheel and waited for impact, for the force to send her beyond the weedy ditch where she'd roll door over door. But it barreled forward and missed her by inches. Hands shot out the windows and waved at her. They were blasting that music and careening toward oblivion. She watched them get small and curve away, and she imagined their future—everyone's future with such hooligans at the wheel, such unfettered depravity. And now she hated the idea of breathing the Plymouth's interior. She cranked the handle down. While the wind fingered at her bun, she spoke to Pastor Whitman, at first mouthing and then speaking in full voice against the windshield. She said that water rolls where it wants only because the righteous refuse to hold it back, because the world is full of its own bustling. Whitman didn't understand because he was a man, a creature of so much flesh and muscle, a body way bigger than the spirit wants. Of course, he was right about time and God, about the constant waiting and the raindrops, but there was Joshua's trumpet, the walls of Jericho—whole cities flattened, whole nations burnt or crumbled. There were ways to push against it all, ways to keep the tide from rolling in over the righteous.

The road curved hard to the right and went on without her. She heard the engine whinny and watched the treeline beyond the field jitter. The steering wheel pounded against her palms until everything went still. Out there beyond her hood, beyond the encroaching dust, the midday clouds were rolling in from Indiana, and Marigold decided that God was there, twisting in the heat above the new corn, that He'd been there all along, and that everyone was moving too fast to see. She decided she would tell Whitman, that she'd explain, best she could, to anyone who'd listen, maybe even the farmer in the distance who was leaving the shade of a sprawling oak and jogging toward her.

The Insult Comic

Since I moved in last summer, I knew Walter was going to get hurt. All along, I imagined some father or boyfriend without a sense of humor climbing the porch steps and knocking Walter in the head. The first time I heard him, I thought he was yelling up at me. I heard shouting through the front window and then laughter—wheezy old man laughter. I sat up straight and waited for another sound to come along and make sense of things. Then I heard, "Holy cow! What's wrong with your head?" which made me get up from the couch, head down the stairs, and peek out the screen. A bunch of school kids were walking past and Walter was launching intermittent attacks.

We've got at least three public crazies in Bryan. There's Disco Dan—a guy who wears a little red cowboy hat and dances his way down the street. People honk and he waves like a president. Then there's Dirty Hank. He's the town drunk. His name is actually Daryl—and he went to school with my Aunt Louise. She says he was just another kid, but something happened along the way, maybe Korea, maybe something worse. Now he's a 50-something falling down drunk with winter boots and one winter coat that he wears all year round. And there's Ralph Wheeler, whose bare chest is a constant part of the Bryan scenery. I've seen him shirtless all the way into November when the rest of us are starting to bundle up. If there were an ocean nearby, he'd make all the sense in the world. But this is Ohio. You can't surf on corn.

I'm guessing that most people see Walter Laney as the fourth town crazy—the only one who's stationary, the one you can walk by like a fountain or a sphinx. He's the old guy at the corner of Cherry and High who abuses everyone within earshot. He's been here for years. People ask me about him. "Don't you live above the guy who yells?" I tell them that I do. I live upstairs. Walter lives down. His ceiling is my floor. In the cold months, I hear nothing. Sometimes it's so quiet down there I wonder if I'll smell the smell you hear about in the movies. Like in most duplexes, we share a front door. Inside, the stairs start right away, so it isn't like we see each other in the hall. When we talk, it's on the front porch—out where bikers, pedestrians, parents with strollers come in and out of Walter's line of fire. If I'm on my way out, I'll take a few extra minutes and sit on the big cement railing while he rocks in the swing. We've had some good talks. I've never gotten him to say much about his life—not until earlier today—but he always asks about mine. I'll be telling him about my work or my family and he'll nod along, adding comments about the nature of things. Then, out of nowhere, he'll snap to attention and blast an insult toward the street. I have to be honest. At first, I was nerved out. But I came to expect it. Then I came to enjoy it. Don't get haughty. You would too.

People walk past and he starts introducing them. "Looky here! It's ol Truckbutt." "Heyho, Gummy!" "Ahoy, Captain Shitcheeks!" And there's one boy he calls Richard Nixon for some reason. What's weird is that kids love it. They'll yell out a response, telling him to shut the hell up or whatever. He claps and laughs like it's the best thing in the world. Sometimes, adults holler back but it's always half-hearted—nothing compared to Walter's bullets. He's got a gift for abuse. And he's not afraid of anyone. Once he asked a couple guys in baseball hats if they were pro players or backyard pansies. "Which is it? It's one or the other." Another time, he asked a thick serious guy in a muscle shirt, "You still peeing the bed?"

"What?" the guy said—even though Walter had said it pretty clearly.

"I say, are you still peeing the bed?"

I tightened, ready for something to start. But the guy pulled his neck back and kept walking. Walter looked disappointed.

Sometimes, he offers advice. "Clean your shoes." "Tuck in your shirt." "Your hair's too flat. Try a perm for God's sake." "Buy a comb. They're only fifty cents." "Holy God, don't wear stripes!" The only time I felt really bad—like I wanted off the porch right away—was when he targeted Mrs. Lambert, who's perfectly nice. "Look out! Look out, everyone," he said. "Big butt coming through. Okay. Just keep on going…easy now…easy." She put her head down and walked a little faster.

So I have to admit that I've been waiting for it. And it happened yesterday. I was upstairs and heard the thumping—like huge shoes in a huge drier. I ran down, opened the front door, and there was Walter balled up in the corner. I saw the two guys heading out of the yard and down the sidewalk. They weren't sticking around and I wasn't going after them. When I went to help Walter up, he clenched. He was bad—bad enough for me to call an ambulance. I sat with him until they came. I watched while they put on a neck brace, slid him onto a flat board, and carted him to the hospital. I wasn't looking forward to my interview with the cops. One of them asked me what I saw and I told him—just two guys walking away. He asked several times if I heard anything before coming out the door. I said no.

Today, I went up for visiting hours. They kept Walter over-night and they're going to monitor him for one more. I peeked in and there he was—with a couple busted ribs, a concussion, and a nice facial rearrangement. That's how he put it.

"You look great," I told him, which he seemed to like. I stood around and wondered what to say. He was watching baseball and didn't seem all that interested in it, so I asked what he said to those two guys.

"Nothing important."

"You think you might ease up on people?" I asked.

"Probably not." He smiled a little—with the unbandaged side of his face.

And here's the thing that kept me around—the thing that made me sit down in the visitor chair for a couple hours. I asked Walter what he used to do. I knew that he'd been in Chicago for a good part of his life, but not why.

"Jesuit," he said. "I'm a Jesuit."

I'd never met a Jesuit or talked to a priest. I wasn't brought up Catholic so I never went to confession or anything. And here was Walter. He told me about Jesuit life. "It's all about the poor," he said. For more than thirty years, he helped poor people in Mex-ico, Peru, San Francisco, and downtown Chicago. He helped people find lost family members, fill out papers for schooling and federal aid. He helped them file complaints against the police after they'd been beaten in the back of a jailhouse. He helped battered women hide themselves and their children from maniac husbands. He sat with people dying of cancer or some unnam-able thing. He stayed with survivors so they wouldn't feel alone even though they were. He attended more funerals than he can remember. He stopped counting the names and ceremonies.

I asked why he left—why he's no longer out there.

"It wasn't for me," he said.

I asked about his family—if he had anyone around.

"Just my sister Clare out at the nursing home," he said. And then he explained, without his usual amusement, how they'd lost their brother, Burt, years back, how Clare took it hard, and then how her husband, a sheriff, shot a man a man on a roof, quit his job, and then disappeared. "She never got her traction after that. Slipped and stumbled through a life mostly," he said. And so now Walter sits with her each morning—when he isn't busted up himself—and talks enough for the two of them.

I asked him how he became a Jesuit. He could've been making it all up, and I don't care either way because it was interesting. Here's a guy who grew up Protestant—Nazarene, which means hard Protestant, as hard as they come around here—who then found his way down the street to the St. Joseph church because, as he put it, there was something foul in the Nazarene air. "Where I grew up," he said, "there were only two paths to salvation—Nazarene or Catholic. The Nazarenes were loons, stark raving fully feathered goddamned loonies. I knew it before I knew anything else." He said all of that with a full throat—loud enough that the patient on the side of the curtain jangled a dish. Walter notched it down but said, like a full confession, that one day when he was no more than ten, he got up in the middle of a hellfire and brimstone sermon, walked out the front door, cruised down the street, and announced himself to the Catholics. They welcomed him, called him a lost son returning home.

He didn't really answer my question, and he knew that I knew it. We watched a few commercials in silence, then I got up to leave. "If there's anything you need," I said, "just let me know."

"Maybe just try walking around up there like you don't have a club foot," he said.

I told him I'd do my best.

The Full Horizon

Back on the mountain, months before bringing his family across the Ohio territory and into the Black Swamp, Jonas Van-Mueller hoped that his wife's grandfather would die. He liked the old man well enough—admired him for the way he could heave a bucket, how his arms and back had conformed to decades of labor, even how he'd work through a bowl of stew at the end of the day. "Leonard," Jonas would say, "you're a testament." And he meant it. He saw Grandfather Leonard as a reminder of the family's good stock, an echo of a bygone age when men and women sliced through hardships of the world. But the trip down the mountain and across the flatland would rattle old bones. It would take weeks—more than a month—before they'd reach the settlement and begin a new life. And for all he meant to Jonas, Maud, and the children, Grandfather was curling in like a dry leaf.

Jonas and Maud never discussed it. Grandfather Leonard would come along to the settlement. After all, there was no one else left. Tuberculosis, age, two farming accidents, and a drowning had taken all the other VanMuellers in the world. They couldn't leave Grandfather on the mountain and they couldn't wait any longer. They had to start early in the spring, roll for four hundred miles or thereabouts, and get seeds into the ground.

Through the last days of winter, as mild air climbed the mountain, Jonas charted out the space. He planned the perfect slot for each bundle, shovel, bag, and crate. He reinforced every bolt and fussed over the hinges. "Are you just fussing?" Maud asked one night. But it was all about movement, Jonas said. If they could avoid attack, injury, and illness, it was simply a matter of getting there. He pictured the wheels turning over miles of sodden earth, cutting through cakey spring mud, coming clean in small brooks. He imagined the continuous rhythm, the pounding of the wood, the daily checks, and critical repairs. He imagined they'd roll for four, close to five, weeks and then finally walk into the settlement to handshakes and revelry. Jonas imagined, too, all the ways that Grandfather might slow the journey—pneumonia, fever, too many stops along the trail, a burial followed by heavy-footed anguish.

But now, here they were more than three weeks away from the mountain, and it was this mammoth swamp, not Grandfather, that had brought them to a standstill. The wagon was leaning like a shipwreck. Everything smelled of rot. The mosquitoes were a constant rumble that made thinking hard.

"Jonas," Maud said.

He looked at her, shin-deep in the murk, her dress wicking the grime up toward her waist.

"Jonas," she said again.

He heard her both times and knew what she meant. But there was so much in the wagon, so many necessities. He sucked in, pressed his eyes shut, and reached down. He wanted to feel something—a rock, a root, the devil's hand, anything that he could pull or pry loose. Grisly slime, nothing solid or fixed, ran through his fingers. And when the mud flowed into his left ear and caulked out the sound above, he surfaced, blew his nostrils clear, and admitted that Maud was right. They would have to leave the wagon behind.

He pulled himself from the socket of mud and led the horses over. "Okay," he said. "Best tie them up. They're all we've got now."

"We'll be alright," Maud said.

He offered a nod, but he knew better. And he knew that she knew better. Without the wagon, they'd have to rely on the gelding and mare to get everyone—all five of them—out of the swamp and another sixty miles beyond it.

He looked at the dry patch where the children stood next to Grandfather, all three waving at mosquito clouds. He watched them watching him, waiting for some decision, for something other than this. He slogged back to the wagon, grabbed the ax, and brought it down against the sideboard. At least they'd get a good fire going.

~

The next morning, Jonas felt Maud roll away. He pushed the blanket back, and the mosquitoes poured around him like noisy air. He followed Maud to the fire. They knelt together, stoked, and blew until the flames came back. He noticed her neck was pocked with welts and that made him want to squish every bug, one at a time, in his fingers.

"Did you sleep?" she said.

"A bit," he said, "between itching."

"They're still asleep."

"Everyone okay?"

"I think so," she said. "I think they're all holding on."

Jonas looked over. Jared, Maria, and Grandfather were breathing through the nets he'd bought from a retired army captain. He wasn't used to seeing their faces screened off, their flesh checkered in gray. And he wasn't used to seeing Grandfather asleep. He'd always been moving, stoking a fire, boiling water before the dim glow of morning. "I don't believe I've ever seen your eyelids," Jonas told him once. "Don't have any," he said back. But now he lay next to the children, a long timber of body, his neck kinked into his sternum, and two eyelids at work.

"Grandfather?" he asked.

"Okay," she said. "I think he's doing okay."

Maud made porridge while Jonas cleaved off another sideboard. The movement, the smell of smoke, and the coming light made his brain turn. He started adding and subtracting. The mare could carry the children, dried fruit, oats, the small satchel, and three bundles. The gelding would take Grandfather, two bundles, saws, and two shovels. Maud could carry the jerky and a small satchel of clothes. He'd carry the lantern, ax, gun, powder, ammunition, and their life savings against his chest. Without the wagon, they'd stay close to the trees where roots firmed up the ground. And they'd veer to the south, where the swamp ended sooner. They'd leave most of the food behind, but there were deer beyond the swamp. Hunger wasn't the problem. Load was the problem. Too much strain and the horses would give out. And then, as Jonas figured it, they'd all be food for this big hungry place.

Maud came to the wagon. "I can take the meat and probably the oats," she said. "The skillet too."

"That skillet's heavy," he said.

"I'll cope."

"I guess we could start out that way."

"Another thing," she said looking back at the fire. "Grandfather wants to walk."

"He'd be standing more than walking."

"I know," she said.

"He'd hold us up."

"I know," she said. "But he won't hear me."

"I'll take a turn at him," he said. And he imagined Grandfather's body—tall and thick with old muscle, a clay giant. Even on solid ground, he moved along like the days of the week.

They packed the bundles high, tied food to the pommels, and let the canteens dangle. Jonas rolled a tarp over the wagon and walked up to the fire where Grandfather stood in a plume of smoke.

"How about you take the gelding?" Jonas said.

"My legs work."

"You're legs work okay."

Grandfather looked at the foggy distance. He crossed his arms and nodded a little.

"I'd be fishing you out every few minutes," Jonas said.

"I got muster left."

"I know you do," Jonas said. "But let's don't spend it on the wrong work."

And that seemed to do it. He'd used Grandfather's own words against him—something he'd been saying for years in Dutch and then in choppy English.

Grandfather gave Jonas a slow elbow and headed for the gelding.

They left the fire smolder. Jonas turned back and saw the wagon conform to the shapelessness around it. He thought of the good hoe, the extra saddle with a firm cantle, and all the cornmeal tucked away. Years might go by before anyone would come along—another party like themselves, a band of Shawnee combing the swamp, or a lone trapper. Some grimy hand—red or mealy white or brown—would pull back the cloth to find rust and decayed leather.

By midday, they'd made three miles at least. And it had been hours since those low moans. Whatever thing made that sound had gone silent or retreated. After bacon and dried fruit, Grandfather played *you say, I say* with the children. Jonas heard a giggle from Jared and he thought of the sky out there beyond the trees. On some sunny morning, they would recall this over coffee and cake. They'd think back to the abandoned wagon and the long-gone rations. They'd remind one another of the mosquito rumble at sunset, how they could barely hear their own voices.

Water surrounded them again in the evening. It started at their ankles and moved up. They almost turned around—veered back north and east—but it had been hours since dry ground—so they waded forward but tacked back and forth. As night came on, the mashing sounds became arrhythmic and sudden. They needed elevation, a slight lift, anything that would provide a camp. Jonas thought of Marten de Graaf, the oldest of all the old trappers who'd spent at least a dozen seasons out in this territory. "You'll be at a crawl," he'd said. "And you won't be the biggest critter in them waters." And Jonas knew that to be true. After first light the day before yesterday, he'd seen a rat or some such thing the size of a pig gliding along, its slime-coated back cutting through the mossy surface.

Behind him in the dark, Jonas heard a splash and turned to a mess of writhing. Maud was up to her shoulders in water trying to lift Grandfather who'd fallen and gone limp. When Jonas got there, the gelding was panicked. It flung him back, and he felt the weight of the ax holding him face-up. He yawed in the murk, rocked to the left, and caught a spongy branch. It broke off in his hand, but he got himself vertical. He grabbed the gelding's bridle and pulled its head down. "Calm now," he said. "Calm now." He kept saying it, getting steadier, until there was nothing but hard breath and dripping sounds.

They strained and heaved until they got Grandfather folded over the gelding's back and tied down. It was pitch dark now. They had no sense of direction. They could only probe along, feeling their way between trunks, waiting for something to brush against their arms. Jonas thought back to the mountain—high above all of this, where the evening sun would cut through the spikes of evergreen—and he wished they'd stayed for another year. He'd said so originally. "Maybe we should let the children thicken up." But the offer to settle new land was too good. The mercantile company needed families, strong men and women who wanted to begin a legacy. It offered huge swaths, protection from Indians, discounts on equipment. Marcus Johnson said he'd personally see to their comfort once they arrived. He guaranteed they'd make it through the first year. "And once you're through the winter," Johnson said, "you'll watch your labors reward you tenfold." Finally, Jonas consented and Maud agreed. And now here they were lunging through unthinkable darkness with no wagon, few supplies, and days from safety. He tried to think of a song or verse to recite, but he couldn't make his brain finger through such things. He was stuck on each step forward, on the hope that his foot would find something higher and harder.

Hours went by. The ground stayed flat and the water stayed deep. When Maud's breath turned to whimpers, Jonas put her on the mare and carried three bundles until one hit a branch and fell away. He kept his head cocked to the left waiting to see first light. He talked to the sun, asked it to hurry along, to quit its moping. He considered the distance—how the light could manage to peek over the ocean, the faraway coast, the mountains back in Pennsylvania, and then swerve past all the trees, how it could keep throwing itself forward and why it would bother. And he tried to remember when he made the decision to veer north—to avoid the Shawnee and slip into the swamp. He'd studied on it for months. He'd listened to all the stories, those that came up the mountain as trappers returned from the flatland. The Black Swamp, they said, was a bad place. "You go in, you stay in." That's what Landon Mitchell said. Others told of fetid air and frantic dreams that would make men wish for wings, gills, or eyes to see behind them. But the younger trappers, those who went out after the war, came back with different tales. They feared Indians. They said the swamp was friendlier than the Shawnee, that tribes to the south were on a rampage. Even children were being tied to stakes and burnt limb by limb. Jonas tried to shove it all away. He knew about people's fears, how they writhe around in the daylight and then thicken when nighttime presses against the windows. He knew that he couldn't abide such fretting. "Worry," he would say, "is its own treachery." Maud vacillated and gave the decision to Jonas.

Grandfather stayed mute until the end—until March when the packing began in earnest. "Our people come from swamps," he finally said. And that made sense.

Jonas tripped on a root, caught himself, and looked back. Grandfather was still folded over the gelding—maybe dead, probably dying. Maud was leaning into the mare's neck and the children were stacked against her. Behind them all, a rose petal glow came through the trees. They'd been moving due west. It meant another two days in the swamp, maybe more. It meant they were still somewhere in the middle, fifteen or twenty miles from the southern rim.

The glow turned into yellow streams, and the distance lit up. Jonas saw slight elevation ahead and to the left. A ridge poked up from the surface.

"Yes," he heard Maud say. "There."

When they reached sod, the gelding's breath turned to cannon sounds. The wet concussions pounded against the giant ribcage and banged into the morning. Its eyes had gone milky, its neck stiff as a wall.

Maud slid off the mare and came to check on Grandfather. Jonas waited for the sound of loss. He let himself hope for it and he worked through the steps that would follow—explaining it to Jared and Maria, erecting a small cross, kneeling on the ground after a long recitation. He charted out the extra space—the lighter load, only the children now to keep from the murk, and a little more food to go around. But there were whispers. There were mumbles and soft questions. In between the gelding's cannon shots, there was an exchange. Maud's head nodded and her arms started working the ropes.

Jonas and Maud wrestled Grandfather's body down. He was mostly awake now but still slack. He oozed over their shoulders and let out yawning vowel sounds. More than once, he got out a full and forceful "no," but they kept hauling and got him seated against a tree.

"Okay," Jonas told him. "Okay now."

Grandfather made a sound like a creaking door. His mouth hung open but his eyes were probing and aware. He scanned Jonas's face, then the patch of sky above them.

"Fire," Maud said. "We need to get him dry."

"Okay."

"Where's the hatchet?"

"On the mare. The small satchel."

When she came back, she told Jonas to bend and lift her up. And he saw her thinking. There were two dead branches low on a craggily oak. He stood against the trunk, hugged it, and pushed his heels up. She shimmied into a stance, her feet grinding into his shoulders. He grunted, pressed his face against the bark, and stayed firm. He felt the hatchet blows vibrate down through her legs and into his jawbone. Then he heard the brittle ends rattle out over the water, and the sound made him feel irreverent, loose, or something else—something that comes along once or twice in a life and then moves on before anyone can name it.

~

The sun warmed Jonas's forehead and the woodsmoke entered his dream—a collage of dinner and breakfast back on the mountain. He imagined that the camp was at peace, that the wagon was nearby, that no one had fallen into the swamp. The cannon sounds had stopped. There was only the crackle of fire. He opened his right eye and saw the mare breathing. And on the ground to his left, the gelding lay dead, its front legs curled up like a mantis, its blood bay hide lit up in the direct sun—a mound of brilliant color, like nothing else for days and nights in any direction.

Maud came up through a helix of smoke, her dress caked with a silt maché. "I figured you should sleep," she said.

Jonas looked at the gelding, then back up at her.

"There was nothing to be done. He just stopped."

Jonas nodded.

"We can walk," she said. "Grandfather and the children can go on the mare."

"The food," he said.

"It can go on the mare."

"We can't overload her."

"We can't stay here," Maud said. "We have to move. This place. It'll be the end of us."

Jonas rubbed a mosquito from his lip.

"Something else."

He waited.

"The powder got wet."

"How wet?"

"Soaked. Must have been when Grandfather fell."

He stared at the gelding's body and thought back to the frenzy. He'd gone completely under. Everything on his back was like the hull of a ship—holding him in place. He didn't think about the powder, only about getting upright, finding his legs again.

"We can eat the meat," Maud said. "If we get it smoking, it could last a while—a few days."

He nodded and looked at the gelding's mass—the solid muscle, the energy lying now in a heap. He looked at the smoky fire, where the children sat dazed and half dressed, Grandfather next to them against a tree.

"Grandfather?" he said.

"Palsy," Maud said. "He can walk a little, not very well."

And Jonas wondered if his face had changed, if Maud knew—the way she knew so many quiet things—that he regretted pulling Grandfather's head from the water during the chaos, that he was waiting for another opportunity, that he wouldn't hesitate if it came.

"Don't let the children watch," he said.

"You'll take some of that meat then?"

"Some. We can take some. But they shouldn't see."

The cutting—the open gash—would tighten everyone up. Even the mare would know. But Maud was right. If the weather stayed cool, the meat would last.

Jonas got the ax and walked along the ridge. He needed to think, find more wood, and get a sense of things. After fifty or so yards, the spongy sod firmed up. There were clumps of deciduous trees—a small kind of maple. Here, not more than a hundred yards away from waist-deep water, from the dark pools they'd waded through hours before—were years of fallen branches, plenty dry as bone, and they made Jonas imagine staying put, building a lean-to, and resting for days. This was possible, he thought. And if the mare could hold out, if she could carry the children and nothing more, they might make it to open land and horizon. And that would be something—to see the sky stop again, to see it all the way around. They were in a bad place, but another week, hardly any time over the course of a life, and they would come into the settlement—winded, delirious from it all, but okay. The little spine of packed earth, in fact, seemed to stretch onward. Maybe they weren't that far, maybe only a few miles from the southern rim. Maybe this spine would lead them in one day's time to open meadows where they could trot the mare, where Jonas and Maud could run along beside her and cover miles and miles in one day and even through the night. It would be safer than staying put. They would whisper along. They would leave the pot, skillet, everything that clanked or banged. They would race through the final hours like spirits, like a passing dream in the sleep of Shawnee children.

That night, Jonas lay down with his face to the fire. He let the heat soak into his forehead and hoped the feeling would last for days. When he was a child, there were stories of people who

could start fires with their eyes. And there were people, too—
not in faraway lands but in his own town, his own family—who
could fly, who could send their souls into the hides of animals or
shadows created by moonlight.

He woke to full sunlight and Maud's voice, warbling and
barely coherent. She'd circled the camp and there was no trace,
nothing. Grandfather was gone. Jonas put his palms on the
ground and let the waves of panic push against him. He reached
back through the hours, through stuttered sleep when he'd
opened his eyes to splintered light and to Grandfather walking
away, looking behind him once, and then continuing until his
silhouette faded into the tree trunks. And Jonas remembered
how the dust was writhing in those first shards of day. Somewhere close, he could tell, the land was dry enough to get picked
up and carried on the wind.

John Mauk grew up on the Ohio flatland. He has a PhD in rhetoric and writing from Bowling Green State University. In 2010, his short collection, *The Rest of Us*, won Michigan Writer's Cooperative Press chapbook contest. His stories have been published in a range of literary journals, and he has been nominated for a Pushcart Prize. He currently teaches at Miami University of Ohio and spends summers in northern Michigan. For more information, visit www.johnmauk.com.